OLIVER
NOCTURNE

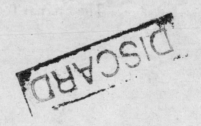

Don't miss a night out with . . .

OLIVER
NOCTURNE

OLIVER
NOCTURNE

THE
DEMON
HUNTER

KEVIN EMERSON

NEW YO...   ...DNEY
MEXICO...   ...AIRES

ISBN-13: 978-0-545-05804-9
ISBN-10: 0-545-05804-X

Copyright © 2009 by Kevin Emerson
Illustrations © 2009 by Scholastic Inc.

12 11 10 9 8 7 6 5 4 3 2 1   9 10 11 12 13 14/0

Printed in the U.S.A.   40
First printing, February 2009

Contents

For W.E.E. who takes me to the zoo...

Prologue

It wasn't his drenched clothing that was making Lieutenant Nick Pederson shake. It wasn't the cold metal of the gun in his hand or the suffocating squeeze of his bulletproof vest. It wasn't even the slight wheezing sound from the corner of the spacious lobby, where his partner, Sarah Laine, lay on the marble floor, her lung punctured by a bullet. . . .

It was what the pimply-faced young man, kneeling on the floor with his hands cuffed behind his back, had just said.

"What are you talking about, Lang?" Nick snapped.

Braiden Lang looked up coldly through his wild curly hair. There was blood on his cheek. "You heard me, Lieutenant," he growled. "The end of the world."

Nick glared at Braiden. "You're a piece of work. We catch you packing the elevators of this building with explosives, you *shoot* my people, and then you try to tell me that you're doing all this to save the world?"

"It's true," muttered Braiden.

The handcuffed man to Braiden's left, his long hair hiding most of his face, chuckled as if Nick were a fool.

A pained cough echoed through the lobby. Nick glanced over his shoulder to where members of his team were busying over Sarah. He felt his blood boil, and leaned menacingly toward Braiden. "You know what I think? I think you and your little group here —"

"We're called the Brotherhood," declared the woman kneeling to Braiden's right. She scowled, contorting the long scar across her left cheek, and stiffened her back importantly.

"Shut up," Nick barked. "I think you're just another bunch of selfish freaks. You're so concerned with your big ideas that you don't even think about who you're going to hurt."

"We're not going to hurt anyone," Braiden mumbled. "We're trying to *save* humanity."

"Oh, right, and we're all going to die if you don't blow up this building."

"Not the whole building, just the top five floors."

Nearby, an antique pewter clock chimed three A.M.

Nick's eyes lingered for a moment, not on the clock, but on the night watchman sitting beneath it, staring out at the lobby with vacant eyes. He wasn't dead, but he was in some kind of trance. Nick and his team had not been able to snap him out of it, but they'd had only a few moments before the shooting began. That brief time had been enough, though, for Nick to notice the two holes in the guard's neck, and the crimson stains on his white collar.

That sight made Nick rub at his own neck. *His* scars were nearly invisible now, but he knew what it felt like to be bitten. He would never forget.

"Just go up to the twenty-third floor," Braiden urged, his eyes flashing to Nick's bite scars. "See for yourself. Part of you already believes me. And we're running out of time. The —"

"Please," Nick muttered, "spare me the talk about a prophecy and some boy who's going to end the world by opening a gate."

"His name is Nocturne," Braiden added calmly, "and he's not just a *boy*. What do you think those are?" Braiden nodded to the piles of silver ash that dotted the marble floor here and there.

"They could be anything," scoffed Nick, yet he had seen ash piles like this before, had in fact *created* one once, with a well-placed wooden stake.

"If the vampires are successful with this ritual tonight, there will be no stopping them," Braiden continued.

"I said . . . spare me." Nick hated what he was thinking. He turned to the two officers behind him. "How's Sarah?"

"We've stabilized her," Officer Williams answered. "Bought her a little time. But —"

"Good. I won't be long." Nick started across the lobby toward the elevators.

"Sir," Williams called after him. "Shouldn't we be calling in the Feds?"

"If I'm not down in five minutes, call them."

"But —"

"That's an order."

Nick rounded the corner. There were three elevators on either side, their doors open. Thick bricks of gray explosive, connected by red wires, had been taped to their gold walls. A female officer knelt inside one car, her cap backward on her head, a pen-size flashlight in her mouth. She was carefully unscrewing the elevator's number panel.

"Any of these defused yet, Alvarez?"

Alvarez cocked her head across the hall. "Only that one. These guys are good."

Nick stepped into the defused elevator and pressed twenty-three. There was a pleasant ding, and the doors slid closed. The elevator rose, tinny Muzak playing.

Nick rubbed at his neck again and wondered about how, in life, the same trouble seemed to find you over and over. After that night long ago, when Nick had first learned the hard way about the vampires in Seattle, the last thing he'd wanted was to have to deal with them again. Yet here he was.

At first, the police had thought that the Brotherhood of the Fallen was a small ecoterrorist cell. Nick had been assigned to find out exactly what they were up to. It hadn't been easy, but when Nick discovered they were hunting vampires, he could only shake his head at fate.

As he dug further, Nick found that, unlike the Brotherhood, the vampires weren't as secretive about what they were doing. They seemed to rely on humans being fairly ignorant, even of things right beneath them. Still, Nick wasn't sure what to make of what he'd learned. Tonight was September 21, the fall equinox. The vampires called it Waning Sun and held large festivals to honor the lengthening of the nights. The Brotherhood thought that the vampires had something extra special planned for this year.

There was a vampire child named Nocturne, who had been marked by a prophecy. The Brotherhood thought that tonight, on the twenty-third floor of this building, the child was going to be given demon power through some kind of ritual. If this was successful, it would mean the end of the world.

But I don't really believe all this, do I? Nick wondered. He didn't think he did, but . . . He had managed to learn a little bit about a vampire organization called the Half-Light Consortium, and while it was unclear exactly what they did, what Nick had learned did seem to confirm what that annoying Braiden Lang fellow was saying.

The elevator slowed and dinged again. Nick took a deep breath. He felt an old ache in his neck. The doors began to slide open.

❋

When Nick returned to the lobby moments later, he already understood that his bright future in the police force was about to come to an end. Maybe he'd get lucky and only get demoted, lose some pay. Or maybe he'd end up in jail. Whatever. He knew what he had to do.

"Pull back, Alvarez," Nick barked as he strode from the elevator.

"But sir, these explosives are still hot."

"That's an order. We're calling in the Feds."

Alvarez huffed, but began to gather her gear.

"Sir, what did you find?" Williams asked as Nick crossed the lobby.

He didn't reply, didn't break stride, until he was beside Williams. Then Nick turned and jumped on Braiden Lang.

"Hey!" Braiden shouted.

Nick said nothing, just punched Braiden in the jaw and wrestled him to the floor.

"What are you doing?" the scar-faced woman snarled, falling back and kicking at Nick.

"Sir!" Williams and the other officers were there in moments, pulling Nick off.

Nick finally relented. "You got that?" he shouted at Braiden, who rolled over on his side, coughing wickedly.

"What is wrong with you?" Williams protested.

"I'm fine," Nick spat, and shook the officers free. "Sorry. He had it coming." Nick glared at Braiden, who returned the cold stare, but didn't say a word.

Nick fixed his tousled jacket. "Williams, keep these vermin covered. I'm taking Laine out and calling in the Feds."

"All right, sir," said Williams tentatively.

Nick turned and walked away, not wanting to think about what he'd just done. Instead, he hurried over to Sarah. "Can we move her?" he asked.

"She's stable," an officer replied.

Nick picked her up carefully and moved toward the door. "Everybody else out!"

They were halfway across the street when gunfire erupted from inside.

"What was that?" shouted Alvarez.

"Take cover!" Nick barked, and broke into a run.

They had just ducked behind their squad cars when the concussion of a massive explosion sent them sprawling. High above, hundreds of windows shattered outward as five elevator cars of explosives detonated on the twenty-third floor.

Glass rained down on them. Nick used his coat to shield Sarah. A mangled office chair crashed onto the roof of the car behind them.

Kneeling there beside Sarah, Nick gazed at her unconscious face, but then had to look away. What had he just done? *I caused the destruction of millions of dollars of property,* he thought. That alone would probably get him in trouble. *But what else did I do?*

He was pretty sure that no one had seen him slip the key to the handcuffs into Braiden Lang's hand as he was pummeling him. He hoped that Lang had the decency to spare his officers' lives as he made his getaway. If nothing else, the explosion meant that Lang had understood what Nick wanted him to do.

After what he'd seen on the twenty-third floor, he'd had no other choice but to let the Brotherhood succeed.

Nick's gaze drifted through the dust clouds and settled on, of all things, a poster on the side of a bus stop. It showed the smiling face of Seattle Mariners superstar Ken Griffey Jr. Nick loved baseball, and the entire city had fallen in love with this year's Mariners team. Would they make the playoffs? Could they win it all? Well, even if it meant the end of his career, Nick knew that

what he had just done would ensure that those questions were answered.

It was 1995, and thanks to Nick, no vampire child
would be ending the world. They'd all be around to see
October, and with a little luck, maybe the Mariners
would go all the way.

CHAPTER 1

Feast of the Dead

As the sun set on the final day of August, Oliver Nocturne awoke and headed out to enjoy his last night of freedom. School started the next evening, and he was not looking forward to it.

Freedom for Oliver was not what it was for most vampires. Though he was sixty-four human years old, he was only thirteen in vampire years, and because he didn't yet have a demon, he was still considered a child.

So freedom was not setting off into the night to stalk and terrorize, as it might be for Oliver's older brother, Bane. It also wasn't heading out to attend a sophisticated party where humans were fed upon, as it might be for his parents, Phlox and Sebastian.

But lately, freedom for Oliver was also not hanging out on his own at home, because his parents were around almost every night. Phlox and Sebastian hadn't gone out to any events like the Friday Social feedings all summer.

Sebastian hadn't stayed late at work as he often had, and Phlox hadn't attended a Central Council meeting in months. Bane had been gone for a few nights at a time now and then, occasionally missing his summer school classes, which put Phlox in a state like nothing else could. Nobody knew what Bane was up to when he was gone, and he wouldn't say. Most nights, though, he returned home as soon as class ended and slouched sullenly on the couch, hogging the TV and video games.

As a result, for the first time he could remember, Oliver was the member of the family who behaved most like a normal vampire, at least when it came to going out at night. But even this freedom was different for Oliver. Other vampire kids would likely be on their way to see some indie bands down in the sewer clubs or at the Vera Project, to mess with human kids on Capitol Hill, or to hang out down at Seattle Center and flirt with the glossy vampires from the east side towns like Bellevue. Oliver's activities, however, were quite different.

That was because Oliver's two best friends — really his only two friends — were not vampires, but instead a human girl, Emalie, and her zombie cousin, Dean. The last thing that the three of them wanted to do was go hang out with the vampires, who would just harass Oliver endlessly about having such friends.

Besides, Oliver, Emalie, and Dean had bigger things

to do. And so, freedom for Oliver was a night like tonight, when they were meeting to plan and plot about the fate of the world.

Oliver left his underground home on Twilight Lane and crossed town in the growing dark. It was only eight in the evening, yet there was no danger of searing sunlight. Earlier in the summer, Oliver would have needed to travel by sewer. Back then, it seemed like summer would last forever, with its tireless daylight and horrid heat. But before you knew it, the shadows were growing longer and darker again, creeping across the street earlier each evening, and the breeze was edged with a coat-buttoning chill.

Oliver's sensitive vampire nose also detected a change in the air. Secretly, the dying that foretold winter had already begun. Sure, the leaves still looked green, but inside, their cells were shutting down processes, closing off paths of energy. The spiders and yellow jackets might have been at their plumpest, like the apples ripening on trees, but that only meant they were soon to fall, or to curl up under a rafter and shrivel away.

As much as Oliver enjoyed the cool darkness, he couldn't shake an ominous shiver in his gut. It seemed silly, but the hints of the changing season reminded him that his future was getting closer. Vampires, as a rule, weren't supposed to worry about the future. Sure, they might feel excited about some coming success, like the outbreak of a war or plague that they'd worked on for many years, but they would never bother to fear what was coming.

Yet Oliver feared his future, because he knew that it involved fulfilling a prophecy to open the Nexia Gate. The Gate was at the center of the universe, and most believed that it held everything together.

From the vampires' point of view, opening the Gate would be a wonderful thing, because it would free their inner demons, the *vampyr,* from Earth, which they thought of as a prison. Where else could you be trapped inside a physical body that could be slain by sunlight or a stake? Where else could you *age* away to dust in just a few hundred years, extinguishing the demon inside forever? If the Gate was opened, the *vampyr* would be freed to roam in the infinite higher and lower worlds for eternity.

Unfortunately, this made opening the Gate very bad for a human, or anything living, and even for Earth itself, because, as Oliver had learned back in June, opening the Nexia Gate would also completely destroy the world. *Oh well,* most vampires would say with a grin. But not a vampire who had human friends and human parents who might be alive out there somewhere.

So, there was going to come a moment when Oliver would have to choose. Maybe it wouldn't be until he was standing in front of the Gate with his demon,

Illisius. And that could be years from now. Or maybe it would be later this fall, during the Festival of Waning Sun, when Oliver was to be imbued with the mystical energy that would allow him to travel to Nexia. Or maybe it would be even sooner than that. The only thing Oliver was sure of was that his future was heading his way, unavoidable as the changing seasons. And he didn't want it.

He entered a wooded park and walked along twisting lonely paths until he reached a ten-foot-high fence, which he easily vaulted over. The Woodland Park Zoo technically closed at eight, and that was the time when the gates were locked and most of the human staff departed. It was also the time when the zoo unofficially opened for anyone who could enter as Oliver had just done.

As he wandered along, Oliver listened to the nocturnal shuffling of the animals, finally free to move about unnoticed. Here and there, hollow calls echoed as a bird, a hippo, or a hyena instinctually searched for others of its kind, its brain unable to completely understand the trap it was in for the rest of its days.

A burst of laughter emanated from the direction of the bug house. Oliver recognized the sound of vampires, and hurried his pace. Now another burst of wild shouting echoed from the savanna enclosure nearby. Oliver was surprised that there were so many vampires here. It was the last night before school, so of course everybody was out. But there were many cooler places to go than the zoo. That was why Oliver had picked it for meeting Emalie and Dean.

Ducking onto a narrow, overgrown path, Oliver continued along quietly in the shadows, hoping to avoid any run-ins with other vampire kids. There had been a time, back in the winter, when Oliver had briefly been considered cool and interesting by his peers. This was because he was the first in his class to have a demon dream, which was a prelude to getting your own demon, and becoming an adult vampire.

Oliver's classmates also believed that he had killed Dean and raised him as a zombie. They still believed this, and they still knew he'd had that demon dream. What had changed since the winter was that his classmates also knew Oliver hung out with Emalie, and being friends with a human was shameful enough to trump anything else.

As spring and summer had passed, Oliver found that he cared less and less what his schoolmates thought of him. Even so, tomorrow night would be soon enough to endure their sneers and taunts.

He rounded a corner and neared the gorilla house. Large panes of glass looked in on the habitat. It was full of ropes and logs for swinging and climbing, yet the gorillas often just sat lethargically in the hay. They, of all the zoo animals, seemed to have the best understanding of their situation as captives.

"Unite us!" a young voice suddenly shouted. Oliver ducked behind a leafy bush, just as a burst of fire ignited next to the windows.

"You dork," chided a high-pitched girl's voice. "Who'd want a gorilla *nahualli*?"

As Oliver spied the two young vampire kids, he cursed to himself. Of course . . . Tonight was the Great Feast of the Dead, a celebration that dated back to the Aztecs and one that vampires loved to honor. Oliver knew about it from history class, which was his favorite subject in school.

The Aztecs had believed that each person had an animal that was a spirit twin, called a nahualli. They'd actually gotten this idea from the vampires among them. Each adult vampire tended to feel a particularly strong connection to one kind of animal, and favored it for Occupation. The vampires living secretly in the Aztec and Mayan communities had used their powers, such as Occupying, to portray themselves as powerful shamans. Then they could wield influence over the people, instigating wars and suggesting innovative new kinds of human sacrifice.

Oliver realized that the reason he'd forgotten about the Great Feast was that his parents hadn't been going out for it. Normally, Phlox and Sebastian would have put on formal clothes and painted their faces with chilling animal designs in blacks, whites, and reds, resembling their favored nahualli. Phlox often chose an owl, Sebastian a crow. They'd have attended a feeding party, where the feast would be unsuspecting humans, likely frozen in Staesys. Yet when Oliver had left the house earlier, his parents had been puttering around like any other night.

Vampire kids also painted their faces to celebrate the Great Feast, but beyond that they could only pretend to occupy the creatures, as real Occupation required a demon.

"You don't know it won't work!" whined the boy. He blew on his hand and a burst of flame ignited from it, shooting out and licking the glass. Oliver caught a scent of singed datura, which was a powerful herb used in many enchantments, especially ones involving *sight* or demon transfer. "Nahualli!" the boy shouted again.

The gorillas looked up with only the slightest interest.

"If *I* were going to have a true nahualli," the girl intoned, "I'd pick something more vicious and noble, like a snow leopard, or a Bengal tiger!"

"Whatever," the boy grumbled.

Oliver ducked back the way he'd come. He wished now that he'd suggested meeting Emalie and Dean somewhere else. But they wouldn't need to be here long, and Emalie could always use her Orani powers to hide from vampire eyes, as she'd done so effectively in Morosia.

Returning to the main path, Oliver was just about to continue on when something else flashed in the corner of his eye. It wasn't a flame, like the kids had been making. For a moment, Oliver hoped it was a firefly — but there weren't any fireflies in Seattle. He remembered back to Italy, where fireflies had seemed to follow him, to lead him, until they spoke as the oracle Selene, who had predicted Oliver's destiny. Selene had transferred her life force into fireflies in order to hide from Oliver's father, who had been sent by the Half-Light Consortium to kill her.

Oliver had summoned Selene in a temple of the dead above the underworld city of Morosia, and she was the one who'd told him that opening the Gate would end the world. She had also tried to tell him that there was a way to undo his prophecy, only she hadn't been able to finish. And now she was gone, killed by Half-Light. Her life force had been used to raise a mystical object called the Artifact, a key part of Oliver's destiny. Whatever Selene had known about freeing Oliver from his fate, it had died with her.

Besides, the light that caught Oliver's eye just now was not that pale firefly green. It had seemed white. He peered into the pine trees, seeing only shadows.

There it was again: some kind of glowing white object, but its exact shape was obscured by the branches and thick trunks. It seemed to shimmer, its edges tinged with silver, throwing off blue sparks, almost as though it were electric.

As Oliver watched, the white glow receded into the woods. He suddenly felt like he wanted, or even *needed* to follow it. The light didn't feel dangerous. In fact, Oliver felt a strange connection to it in the forces around him: It almost seemed familiar.

He moved off the path, treading quietly. For a moment, he lost sight of the light completely, but then spied it again. It seemed to be drifting along in no hurry.

Oliver weaved more rapidly through the trees. He closed on the shape. It looked narrow, tall. Not a figure, exactly, but the word *apparition* came to mind.

An apparition was an energy concentration, almost like an echo of someone or something. It was different than a wraith, which was a person's spirit that was still attached to this world by grief. Apparitions wouldn't be able to act or speak in this world. They were thought to be *drawn* by a person, meaning that they weren't just beings on their own, but were created by the people who saw them. Like a memory made real. Was that what this was? Oliver needed to get a better look.

The light winked out. Oliver blinked, turning his head about. Where had it gone?

Then he walked into a brick wall. It was chest high, and his knees and torso thumped against it. He stumbled back, annoyed, but spied the light again on the other side. It was about twenty feet away. As he watched, it seemed to lower and sink out of sight.

Oliver leaped easily over the wall and found himself in a cleared area beneath tall pines. The ground was covered with wood chips. Slides for small children had been carved into large rocks. In front of him was a series of concrete mounds with tunnels running beneath them. Oliver approached the nearest entrance. A short flight of stairs led down into the passages. Bending over, Oliver caught another glimpse of the white light. It didn't seem to be moving.

It's waiting for me, he thought, and felt like that was true.

"Hello?" Oliver whispered. He ducked and dropped down the steps. The apparition hovered just beyond a bend in the passage. Oliver moved slowly toward it. He thought he could make out some features now in the blue-white light: arms, legs, a head, and hair.

Hey . . . Oliver heard a voice in his mind, weak and distant, and he felt sure that he recognized it. But apparitions weren't supposed to be able to speak.

Oliver tried to make out the face, but couldn't. He needed to get a little closer, see the apparition fully, and talk with it. He really wanted to know what it was . . . but something froze him in his tracks.

There was a new sound in the dark: a deep, guttural growl. The apparition began to fade, its light dissolving.

"Wait!" Oliver whispered after it.

The growling increased. It vibrated like a car engine. Oliver looked around, then up.

Above him was a hole in the concrete ceiling, and peering over the edge of this space was a giant, feline face with glowing black eyes. Oliver scrambled backward, falling. The creature hissed, baring a mouth of razor-sharp teeth, and lunged at him.

Thick paws slammed against Oliver's chest. The weight of the creature pinned him to the ground, its spotted face filling his vision. Whiskers brushed against his cheeks. A drop of hot saliva dripped into his eye. The cat unleashed a piercing cry, its sour breath blasting Oliver's face. Its glowing black eyes bore into him. Oliver could also smell a pungent but familiar odor.

Suddenly the cat was enveloped in black, swirling smoke. It leaped off Oliver. He sat up to see a figure appearing. Before he could make out who it was, he recognized the laughter.

"Ha! What a *lamb*!"

Oliver scowled. "Shut up, Bane."

Bane crouched in front of Oliver, a wicked grin stretching the painted pattern of black and red spots that adorned his bone-white face. That gross smell was the coyote and aniseed cologne that he'd been drowning himself in lately.

Behind him, the dazed cat turned to dash off. "Stay, little nahualli," Bane said and flicked his wrist, tossing a tiny glass sphere. It hit the wall beside the cat and exploded in a puff of dust. The cat seemed to choke, then slumped to the ground and lay still, chest heaving slowly, its eyes open, its body paralyzed.

"What a creature, eh?" said Bane. "We're demon twins."

"Whatever," Oliver muttered. "Like you could have a jaguar nahualli. They're supposed to be noble —"

Bane socked Oliver in the shoulder. "That's for being dumb!" He glared darkly at Oliver, but then grinned again. He brushed his long bangs, dyed with shocks of green, from his face. "And you should have seen the look on your face! You'd think it would get old, bro, but it never does."

"Yeah, it sure is funny," Oliver mumbled, as he got to his feet.

Bane's arm shot out, knocking Oliver down again. "Watch your mouth, dork."

Something clattered like claws on the top of the

tunnels. Oliver looked up to see a wolf peering down at them. Now a black bear appeared. These animals also had glowing black eyes.

"Hey, gents," Bane said to the animals. Black smoke swirled around them, and Bane's friends Ty and Randall appeared. Their faces were also painted with designs in skeletal colors. They produced glass spheres and incapacitated their animals. "Look what I found," Bane continued. "What should we do with him?"

Randall's grin faded. "How about I tear his limbs off?" He sounded like he meant it, and Oliver saw Randall flexing his right hand. His arm had been burned off by the Scourge of Selket back in the winter, and had only recently finished regrowing. Emalie was responsible for Randall's injury, although she'd been possessed at the time. Randall blamed Oliver, because the Scourge had been meant for him. The Brotherhood of the Fallen had been trying to slay Oliver so that he wouldn't open the Gate.

"Or," said Bane, "we could drop him in the hippo pool. That'd be fun to watch."

"Why don't we go do something that's not completely boring?" grumbled Ty.

"Good point," Bane agreed. "Anyway, we wouldn't want to damage the favorite son."

"Better than being the shame of the family," Oliver shot back before he could stop himself.

Bane's eyes narrowed to slits. "Excuse me?" Oliver saw his brother's fingers tighten into a fist.

Don't say anything else, Oliver thought, and yet, since he'd confronted his father in Italy, Oliver was finding that it helped to try to say what he was feeling. At the time, he'd thought that his parents were so ashamed of him that they were going to slay him and start over with a new son, but when he finally confronted his dad, he'd found that their feelings were quite different.

"Big deal," Oliver said. "So you can push your little brother around. You're just jealous because I have a destiny." Oliver felt strange using his destiny as a weapon against Bane, since Oliver didn't even want it. In fact, Bane would have been much better suited to the prophecy. Ending the world wouldn't bother him one bit, and he'd probably love all the attention of being the chosen vampire. Still, it was all Oliver had to fight back with. "And what do you have?" he continued. "Some fancy new Occupying powers, so what."

"Oh yeah?" Bane had Oliver by the shirt in moments and hurled him up out of the tunnels. Oliver spun through the air, trying to find the forces, but slammed to the ground, his back spiking with pain. As he tumbled down the side of one of the cement mounds he thought that, while this whole saying-what-you-were-feeling thing might be good in the long run, in the short term it seemed to lead to pain.

Oliver landed on his stomach, getting a mouthful of wood chips. Bane vaulted out of the tunnel and stalked toward him.

"Hey, Bane, can we go already?" called Ty, his voice flat with boredom.

Bane's eyes glowed fiercely. "Don't talk to me about your destiny, you miserable butt fungus."

Oliver jumped to his feet. "Leave me alone."

"I should," Bane snarled, but he paused. "If you had any idea . . ."

"About what?" Oliver was surprised to hear himself shouting, but he couldn't help it. "What am I too much of a *lamb* to know about now? *You're* the one who doesn't have a clue. You've been digging around all year trying to find out more about my destiny 'cause you wish you had it!"

"Ha!" Bane spat, eyes burning, but he stayed rooted in place. "Don't act like you know anything, bro. 'Cause you don't, you really, *really* don't." Bane's voice cracked a little, from anger, Oliver guessed.

"Can I rip his leg off?" Randall called. "Or can we just leave?"

Bane glared at Oliver. Oliver stared back, trying to keep his eyes narrowed, trying not to let his legs buckle. Bane seemed even more angry than usual.

Finally, Bane spun and returned to his friends. "We're outta here," he barked, dropping down into the tunnel.

Ty and Randall stood and dissolved into smoke swirls, then rushed back into their animals. The wolf and bear got to their feet and were joined by the jaguar. The three grunted and growled to one another, then took off as a pack into the trees.

Oliver felt the dizzying rush of his nerves unwinding. That had not been fun. Not that things had ever been particularly fun with Bane, but lately they seemed even worse. Bane wasn't happy about summer school, even though it allowed him to finally catch up on his studies like Occupying, which his friends had learned back in the spring. He always seemed irritable, and kept to himself even more than usual. It had been a long time since he'd come home and shared stories of his exploits with Phlox and Sebastian, as he once had.

Then again, they were still mad at Bane for getting the family kicked off the boat to Isla Necrata, which was a major embarrassment, not to mention that it cut their summer vacation short.

Bane had been caught stealing the summoning charm for Selene, when Half-Light was still trying to acquire it. Oliver didn't know whether Bane had used the charm during the time that he'd had it. Had he summoned Selene, and if so, what had he learned about Oliver's prophecy? And why had he wanted to summon her in the first place? Was it really for the simple reason that he was jealous of Oliver? Or was it more than that?

Maybe he really is jealous, and trying to find a way to get my destiny for his own.

Whatever Bane was up to, Oliver hadn't heard his parents talk about it much at all. Overall, there seemed to be a lot of *not* talking this summer when it came to Bane. Since the trip to Morosia, it was almost as though Oliver and Bane had switched places.

Well, hopefully Bane was out of his hair for the night, and he could get back to meeting up with Emalie and Dean. Oliver hurried across the zoo to the echoing sounds of lonely animals and vampires at play. He kept to the shadows, and kept an eye out for that strange apparition, but it didn't appear again.

Chapter 2

Bats and Bodies

Near the center of the zoo was a long, low building. Half of it contained reptiles, and the other half held the nocturnal animals exhibit. Oliver passed the main entrance and reached a maintenance door. It had a thick padlock, but that was only for show. The lock had been specially made with a release button on the back, placed there by a thoughtful vampire employee.

The room was comfortably warm, lit only in low red. Oliver was relieved to find that there weren't too many vampires around. He passed a group of three kids sitting on the rocks inside the turtle habitat, snickering softly to one another, silhouetted in the red light. A group of younger girls knelt in a circle on the floor, tossing dice made of bone.

Oliver kept his head down as he passed the vampires, only looking up to gather the curious glances from the reptiles, who were busy and alert with nighttime activity. They had sensitive noses and were aware of the forces, too, so vampires intrigued them in ways that annoying humans never could.

At the end of the reptile hall, Oliver pushed through a set of double doors and wound his way into the nocturnal animals room. Day and night had been switched for these creatures so that humans could see them at their most active. At ten P.M. the lights would be turned on for the rest of the night, but Oliver had a little time in the dark before that. He walked on a twisting catwalk with angled glass walls looking in on the dark habitats. He noticed a slow loris creeping by, and heard the rustling of an anteater on the simulated forest floor below.

He stopped at the last habitat and sat down on the carpeted floor, elbows around his knees. Despite his side trip with the apparition and his brother, Oliver still had a few minutes before Emalie and Dean would arrive.

In front of him was a display of trees with thick ropes strung in between. There was movement, and then the ropes began to twist and bend — a flapping of leather — and now a small creature approached, pulling its way along a rope: a vampire bat.

The creature reached the glass, its upside-down head peering out at Oliver, its nose twitching about.

"Hey," said Oliver quietly. The bat continued to survey him as he stood and produced a small plastic bag from his sweatshirt pocket. He placed his other hand against the glass. The bat reached out, touching the tiny elongated fingers at the end of its leathery wing to the glass where Oliver's hand was.

"Maybe you'd be my nahualli," Oliver said quietly. Unlike a jaguar or tiger, the little vampire bat was never going to be the symbol of an army or a great leader. It preferred the shadows, where it could be less noticed as it went about its existence. Oliver liked that.

He concentrated on the forces and levitated a few feet off the floor, until his head was just below the ceiling and his face was even with a tiny, grated air vent.

The bat clambered up into this corner. With amazing dexterity, it reached out and peeled the grating away from the hole. "Thanks," said Oliver.

He reached into the bag and removed a gorged Malaysian mosquito. It was enormous by mosquito standards, about an inch across. Holding it carefully by one of its delicate legs, Oliver held it through the hole. "Fed on wild pigs, like you like," he added quietly.

The vampire bat sniffed at it, then grabbed the blood-filled insect and loped away along the rope. Now, a second bat arrived, swinging along the ropes by its feet. A third followed not far behind.

A feeling of calm spread through Oliver. He liked to watch the bats cradle the fat insects in their fingers, their noses inspecting the prize, and then carefully eat. They were as complicated a creature as any, and Oliver wondered if these three worried about their futures, or pondered their existence. Did they even know they were in a cage? If they did, did it bother them? Or did they think that this cage was their entire world, and if so, what did they think of it? Maybe they thought it was just fine, because it was all they knew. Oliver wondered if that was really so bad.

He fed the second bat and was pulling the last insect from the bag — when every light in the exhibit turned on.

The bats shrieked.

Oliver's vision exploded into static white. He lost track of the forces and tumbled to the floor. What was going on? The lights weren't supposed to come on for another —

The double doors crashed open.

"Jennings and Blake securing the night room, sir!" a voice barked.

Oliver rolled onto his back, blinking madly, but the world around him was little more than faint gray lines drawn in white.

Booted feet clomped up the ramp. He could smell the humans. They would reach him in moments. The bats shrieked urgently, advising Oliver to flee. He was still confused — yet now there was a new, familiar scent.

Just past the vampire bat exhibit, the exit door slammed open.

Oliver rolled until he hit the side wall of the catwalk, then shut his eyes tight and tried to concentrate. He had to spectralize now.

More footsteps. A human approached, his breathing thin, his heart rate high.

Oliver finally reconnected with the forces and began to sink back from the world. Would it be soon enough? He tried opening his eyes again. They'd adjusted enough that he could make out some colors and shapes in the overwhelming brightness. There was the human, in a brown jacket, a gun raised in one hand, a radio in the other.

"Anything, sir?" a voice crackled from it.

"Nothing yet," replied Detective Nick Pederson as he moved slowly along the catwalk.

He was practically beside Oliver when there was a loud thud that made the detective jump. One of the bats had lunged against the glass right beside him. It hissed wickedly. Detective Pederson swore to himself.

In that instant of distraction, Oliver got to his knees and, keeping himself spectralized, scrambled to the ceiling, then down the hall until he reached the exit door. He glanced back, saw that the detective was continuing down the catwalk, and slipped around the corner.

He hung down to push open the door when it was yanked open. A head appeared right in front of him.

"Dude!"

"Tsss!" Oliver darted back, lost his traction, and fell to the floor. He looked up to see Dean and Emalie peering in. Dean was in his usual long coat, his matted hair sticking this way and that. Emalie's hair was in braids, and she wore a denim jacket.

Dean couldn't resist chuckling at Oliver's sprawled position. "Nice."

Emalie elbowed Dean. "Oliver," she whispered. "Come on."

Oliver scrambled to his feet and ducked out the door, following Emalie and Dean down the walkway to a larger path. Red lights flashed in the trees. "What's going on?" Oliver asked.

"Lots of police," reported Dean, "but we're not sure why yet. We were just about to come in and meet you when they showed up."

As they crept along the path, Oliver fell into step with his friends. They reached a wide intersection and saw a commotion up ahead. There were police cars and an ambulance, their engines off but their red and white lights still flashing. A news truck was backing into position, a large floodlight raised high above it, its beam falling on a female newscaster. She stood by the glass wall surrounding the penguin habitat. Most of the action seemed to be focused there.

Oliver caught a scent on the wind. He turned to Dean, who met his gaze with a knowing raise of the eyebrows.

They got as close as the shadows would let them, then ducked and rushed to the side of one of the police cars. Peering over its hood, the three could see through the glass wall of the penguin habitat, to the little rock island surrounded by a moat of water.

That was where the body was.

Emalie's breath caught in her throat. The body lay on the very top of the island, sprawled faceup, arms and legs dangling down. Penguins stood motionlessly about, some staring at the corpse like mourners, some at the activity around them, as if they were appalled by the humans' lack of respect.

Oliver sniffed at the air, and from the molecules of scent spreading on the breeze, he knew the death had been recent.

"Looks like a boy," whispered Dean, "A little older than us?"

Oliver nodded. "Lots of blood around his neck . . . And . . ." His nose reported another disturbing fact, and he turned to Dean again. "You smell that?"

"Yeah," Dean replied. "An animal . . ."

"An animal did this?" Emalie asked incredulously.

"We are in a zoo," said Oliver. "And . . ." He realized that he knew the scent from moments before: the jaguar.

"Heads up," said Dean. "There's good ol' Detective Pederson."

The detective was emerging from the doors to the reptile room, flanked by officers. He approached the penguin enclosure and was greeted by two women, one younger with a badge and gun on her belt, the other older and stocky. As the three converged, Oliver and Dean trained their sensitive ears, and Emalie reached out with her mind to listen.

"Hey, Sarah," Pederson said to the other officer.

"Hey, Nick," Sarah replied. "This is Marion Burke, the zoo director."

"Are you in charge?" Marion asked worriedly.

Nick glanced at Sarah before he replied. "For the moment, but —"

"Okay, you've *got* to get your people back to this location and let my staff lead the search. Sasha is not going to be easy to find and care needs to be taken —"

"Sasha is the least of my concerns," muttered Nick ominously.

"Nick —" Sarah interrupted.

Nick frowned. "All right." He pulled out his radio. "I

need all units back at the penguin enclosure immedi-ately." He turned back to Marion. "You have your team meet me over by that squad car in two minutes."

"Okay." Marion turned and flipped open a cell phone.

Nick strode ahead, Sarah falling into step beside him.

"That's the guy who was working with the Brotherhood in the winter?" Emalie whispered.

"The one and only," said Dean.

Detective Pederson had reached the penguin enclo-sure and was gazing in at the body. Oliver listened intently as Sarah leaned in.

"Care to tell me how you happened to get here so quickly?" she asked seriously.

"It's better if you don't know," Nick replied grimly.

"But what if I can guess, Nick? This is about your vampires, isn't it? So what am I going to tell the lieuten-ant when he arrives?"

Nick glanced at her, looking hurt. "*My* vampires?" He shook his head. "Look, I don't know, tell him I was just driving by."

"Oh come on," Sarah said. "If I have to cover for you again, then you could at least tell me what we're dealing with."

"I'm not sure yet, but it's not your average animal attack."

"You don't think the jaguar did this?" Sarah asked.

"Not *just* the jaguar."

"Detective!"

Nick and Sarah both glanced back to see the TV reporter striding toward them, microphone held out like a magic wand, her hair blond and perfect. Oliver recognized her. She was actually a vampire named Karma Kayne.

"Great," Nick grumbled.

There was a commotion beyond the cars, and Oliver saw a team arriving with tranquilizer rifles.

More sirens echoed in the distance.

Dean nudged Oliver. "We should get out of here before we get caught, or shot."

They ducked back to the shadowed safety of the nearest path.

"What was all that about vampires?" Dean asked.

"The detective thinks the jaguar was Occupied when it killed that kid," Oliver explained.

"Why would a vampire kill a human like that?" Emalie wondered aloud.

Oliver shrugged. "Well, it's not considered the worst thing to kill humans," he said. "But it is frowned upon, especially doing it in a public way like this. It calls too much attention to the vampires."

"What happens to a vampire who does something like this?" asked Emalie.

"I don't know. They'd maybe get fixed with a binding enchantment, like house arrest, for a couple years, or something."

"That's it?" Emalie exclaimed. "For killing someone?"

"Well, yeah. That's just how vampires see things," Oliver replied defensively. "It's not like I'd be out there killing humans."

"I know," Emalie said.

"But there's a bigger problem," said Oliver. "I saw Bane earlier tonight, and he was Occupying the jaguar."

"Whoa, dude," said Dean. "You think Bane did this?"

"I don't know. No, but . . . maybe? He was in a pretty bad mood last time I saw him. Not to mention all summer." Oliver actually felt a sliver of worry for Bane. He was already in enough trouble. He wouldn't go and do this, would he? Then again, who could ever tell what was going on in Bane's head? Still, it seemed irresponsible, even for him. And there had been a lot of vampires in the zoo tonight. It could've easily been someone else. "He might have just been stupid and forgot to close the cage, or left the jaguar out somewhere. And there's no way the detective could know for sure that the jaguar was even Occupied. He'd have to test the blood for force signatures. And there's no way he knows how to do that."

Dean started up the path. "We should leave from the north entrance, away from those hunters."

"Nnn . . ."

Dean and Oliver turned to find Emalie standing stiffly, her eyes shut tight, wincing. "What?" Oliver asked.

"His name was Dante . . ." said Emalie, her voice shaking. "Band . . . he was in the band . . . drums . . . snuck into the zoo with his friends, stopped to tie his shoe . . ." Her voice was hitched with fear. "Orange eyes. It dragged him, scraping on the ground, then . . . His mom didn't know he was here." Emalie's last words dissolved into a long exhale. Her eyes opened. She looked at her hands. "White now, quiet." She shuddered and wrapped her arms around herself.

Oliver had seen this happen to Emalie before, back in Italy when she'd connected with the spirit of a murdered security guard. A person's spirit apparently stayed around its fallen body for a little while, before slowly drifting off and finding a gateway out of the world.

Oliver wondered about the apparition he'd seen earlier. Had it been someone's spirit? Maybe those two ideas were connected somehow.

Emalie let out a quavering sigh. "I'm fine," she said, and caught up with Oliver and Dean. The three headed up the path toward the exit.

Oliver glanced at Emalie. She looked pale, shaken. He reached over and attempted to rub her shoulder supportively, except that his body immediately tensed with nerves, and he was overrun with ridiculous thoughts: *Don't rub too hard! Or too long! Wait, on the shoulder or arm? Yes, shoulder! No, on her back! No not the back! Wait but —*

He ended up patting her shoulder twice and then retrieving his hand. She looked over and almost smiled.

"That kill was consistent with what jaguars do," Dean said randomly. "Bite to the neck, dragging the kill to a high, secluded spot to eat later . . ." He looked up and found both Oliver and Emalie staring at him. "What?" he said. "I like that predator/prey stuff."

They were winding through a heavily wooded section of the path when Oliver paused. "Wait," he whispered. Emalie and Dean stopped.

Oliver sniffed the air and found the faintest trace of that noxious smell: Bane's coyote musk and aniseed cologne. He listened carefully, but there was only the rustling of trees in the breeze. Besides, the scent was very faint.

He glanced around to be sure — and spied something on the ground. He stepped to the edge of the path. There, among the leaves and dirt at the base of the bushes was a small object: a pendant on a leather strap.

One end of the leather had a little hook. The other end was missing, only frayed leather remaining, as if it had been torn free.

Oliver picked up the necklace. It reeked of Bane's cologne.

"What is that?" Emalie asked.

"Weird. I think it's Bane's," said Oliver. "Maybe it fell off when he was playing jaguar."

Oliver studied the pendant. It was a square of magnetite, with a Skrit symbol carved in the middle and painted white:

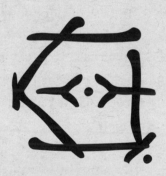

Oliver didn't recognize it. "Knowing Bane, it's probably some gross love charm or something."

"Or maybe it has something to do with whatever Bane's been up to," Emalie suggested. "You know, with Selene and your prophecy."

"Could be." Oliver dropped the necklace in his pocket. "Maybe it can explain some things, since he never does."

"You can use it to blackmail him, if nothing else," Dean suggested with a cautious grin.

"Mmm," Oliver agreed.

They walked on, reaching the entrance gate. Oliver and Dean each took Emalie by an arm, and they vaulted over it as a trio. They crossed a parking lot and entered a small park.

"What were we meeting up for tonight?" Oliver asked blankly.

"Oh yeah," said Dean, stopping in the sandy play ground area. "Duh, we were going to hit another graveyard. Emalie updated the map."

"Right." Emalie reached into her shoulder bag and produced a beat-up city map. They'd been using it to keep track of their progress searching graveyards for Oliver's human parents. Howard and Lindsey Bailey had been killed on the same night that Oliver had been sired, or turned into a vampire from a human. Oliver had been an infant at the time, in the year 1946. Emalie had found an obituary for the Baileys, but it didn't say where they'd been buried.

Then there was the troubling fact that Braiden Lang had told Oliver that his human parents were really alive. There was no proof of that either, but Oliver wanted it to be true. Over the summer, the three had searched online in local records, and then across the country, for a living Howard and Lindsey Bailey who were the right age — Oliver figured they'd be at least eighty — but they weren't out there, at least not under that name.

Not knowing what else to do, they'd started searching the graveyards in town. This search was as much *not* to find them as to find them. If they weren't buried anywhere, that helped somewhat to prove that they were alive. Of course, there was the possibility that the Baileys weren't even buried in Seattle. They could be anywhere. Oliver knew the whole thing was a long shot, yet it was all he could do, and he felt he had to do something.

"Okay, here . . ." Emalie was just unfolding the map when her eyes rolled up in her head, eyelids fluttering. Her knees buckled and she slumped, falling backward. Oliver and Dean reached belatedly for her. Her shoulder slapped a swing as she toppled to the sand.

Oliver and Dean were beside her in a moment. Her eyes had closed. "Emalie," said Oliver. "Hey, Emalie!"

"Nnn . . ." She winced, then her eyes slowly creaked open. "What happened?"

"Don't know," said Dean. "You just checked out."

Emalie pushed up onto her elbows. "Oh . . . Probably just from the spirit encounter back there. Sometimes it's a little intense."

"This has happened to you before?" Oliver asked, sounding like a concerned parent.

"Maybe, yeah," Emalie said. "Once or twice. I'll be fine. Just gotta get a Slurpee or something."

"You should rest," insisted Dean. "No grave searching tonight."

Emalie started to stand. "Nah, I'm good, I —"

She collapsed again, only this time Oliver and Dean caught her.

"Dean's right," said Oliver as they hoisted her to her feet. "Home. You're the only living person here, and we're keeping it that way."

"Come on, you guys. It's not that bad," said Emalie, but she didn't sound convinced.

"We can look again next weekend," said Oliver, trying not to sound as worried as he was. It was very rare for a human to interact with spirits of the dead like Emalie could. Even powerful Orani were only known for their ability to read the minds of the living.

Once Emalie was back in her room, Oliver and Dean skulked around town for a while, trying to enjoy this last night of freedom, but they found themselves strangely quiet.

"Not a bad summer," Dean said at one point. "There were those Charion rides . . ." When Oliver didn't chip in with his own summer recap, Dean went on. "And that night when Ty let us help out in the ice cream truck."

Oliver was able to wrench himself out of his thoughts to add, "And the night we broke into the supermarket with Autumn."

"Y-yeah," Dean said, his voice cracking awkwardly at the mention of Autumn Fitch, who was a zombie and one of Dean's homeschool classmates. Her mother, Ariana, was their teacher.

Neither Dean nor Oliver had been able to carry the conversation after that. A few blocks later, Dean said, "You're worried about her."

"Aren't you?" Oliver replied.

"Well, yeah," said Dean. He sounded relieved to admit it. Oliver felt the same way. "Her powers seem to be getting to her. And I mean, she's only human . . ."

"We'll have to keep an eye on her," said Oliver.

They both fell silent again.

Eventually, they gave up and headed home. Oliver's thoughts about the events at the zoo, with both Bane and Emalie, kept him awake long past dawn.

CHAPTER 3

The Odd New Normal

The next evening, Oliver found himself standing by his coffin, scowling at the black tie in his hands. He'd already put on the white button-down shirt and black pants that were his school uniform, but slipping the tie around his throat would somehow make it official. He thought ahead to the night of school to come, his last year of Eighth Pentath, which was like the end of seventh grade, and could imagine nothing good about it.

Upstairs, the booming, urgent voices of newscasters told him that Phlox had flicked on the television in the kitchen. Oliver tossed on the tie and grabbed his backpack. It was empty and feather light, likely for the only time this year. He wanted to get upstairs to see if there'd been a report on the jaguar attack —

"Oliver."

Oliver almost jumped. Sebastian was leaning out of the bathroom, wearing black silk pajamas and slippers. "Can you give me a hand with this?"

A long silver cylinder was attached to his left elbow. Inside this metal tube, Sebastian was regrowing the forearm and hand that he had lost back in June. The loss of his arm was the price for wielding the Stiletto of Alamut, a mystical weapon that he'd used to try to kill Selene.

"Sure," Oliver replied, faking enthusiasm. He still wasn't used to having his dad around during the nights. Normally, Sebastian would be away at work as an attorney for Half-Light before Oliver woke up, but with his injury he'd been working from home all summer.

Sebastian retreated to the sink. "I just need help changing the solution," he muttered.

Oliver didn't like this. He'd never considered the possibility that his dad could be vulnerable to anything, or a failure. Sebastian had always been so in control, so capable, the imposing figure in the fine suit, sweeping in and out on important business. Now, he was stuck in the house, perpetually wearing pajamas, his face weary from the constant pain in his arm. As long as he was wearing the cylindrical regrowth chamber, he couldn't Occupy, evanesce, or spectralize. Basic levitation was even difficult.

Oliver joined his dad by the sink and took hold of the cylinder. With his remaining hand, Sebastian unfastened two latches at the top. "Hang on to it," Sebastian instructed, then tapped a small keypad. The cylinder unlocked and widened with a hiss. Oliver slowly lowered it, revealing the beginnings of Sebastian's new limb: a skinny, glossy white forearm, still miniature in size, extending down from his elbow and ending at a tiny hand with barely formed fingers. Steam rose off it as the growing solution evaporated.

Oliver turned his gaze from the sight as quickly as he could, instead concentrating on pouring the scalding-hot, orange liquid from the cylinder down the sink. He turned back to see his father gazing forlornly at the stunted new limb.

Sebastian caught Oliver watching him, attempted a smile and said, "It still has some way to go, doesn't it?" He held out his normal hand, and Oliver gave him the cylinder.

They moved to the counter, where a glass flask of golden liquid sat beside two bowls of crystal powders. Oliver dutifully added the powders to the cylinder, and then poured in the liquid. A burst of steam erupted from the cylinder as the solution formed. He opened the medicine cabinet and removed a small black bottle shaped like a snake's head. He twisted off the cap, revealing a dropper tip. Sebastian held out the cylinder and Oliver tapped the bottle, releasing two drops of Krait venom into the solution, which helped to numb the growing pains.

Sebastian lowered his new arm into the cylinder,

wincing as it entered the solution. "Dr. Vincent says it's coming along on schedule," he said sullenly, "but it will still be awhile."

"Mmm," Oliver replied.

Vampires were quick healers. An injury that might kill a human, like a stabbing or a gunshot, would heal in a matter of weeks. Oliver had broken his jaw back in Italy, and while it had seemed to take forever to heal, it had really only been a few days. Even so, Sebastian's new arm was still going to need another month to fully regrow.

The cylinder hissed as it closed. Sebastian snapped the top clips into place, then typed on the keypad. A red light flipped to green. "Thanks," he said, and reached awkwardly to ruffle Oliver's hair. He would normally have used the other hand. "Looking forward to school?" Sebastian asked as they both left the bathroom.

"Sure," Oliver replied flatly.

Sebastian chuckled at Oliver's lack of conviction. "I didn't get to hear about your last night of summer. Did you do anything for the Feast?"

"Not really," Oliver began, but hesitated. It was still hard to get used to telling his dad the truth about his activities. He'd spent the entire winter and spring hiding the fact that he'd been hanging out with Emalie, as his parents had been quite open about their disapproval of his human friend. They hadn't minded him hanging out with Dean, because they'd thought that Oliver was Dean's master. Oliver's parents now knew otherwise, because it had been Dean, under orders from his true master, a young vampire with a demon named Lythia LeRoux, who had thwarted Sebastian's attempt on Selene's life.

"I met up with Emalie and Dean at the zoo," said Oliver, still fretting inside at saying Emalie's name aloud. He was worried about what his parents thought of Dean now, too. After they'd found out he was Lythia's minion, Oliver had expected them to forbid him from seeing Dean, but they hadn't. Maybe they weren't worried about Lythia anymore. Or maybe they were watching carefully whenever Dean was around. Oliver found himself doing that with Dean, now and then.

"Oh? Did you have a good time?" Sebastian asked, his tone mild, but not exactly enthusiastic.

"It was okay."

Sebastian and Phlox probably wished that Oliver wasn't hanging out with a zombie and a human at all, but they seemed to have decided, at least for now, to accept it. Oliver was, after all, different from every other vampire child, and so maybe he should be allowed to act differently.

Oliver was the only child who had ever been sired from a human. All other vampire children had been created from the DNA of their parents and grown in a special lab. It was supposed to be impossible to sire a child, because siring involved merging a human with a *vampyr* demon. Children were not strong enough to be inhabited by a demon until they reached their later teen years.

In the tens of thousands of years of vampire history, Oliver was completely unique in two ways: He was a child who had been sired, and he was a sired vampire without a demon. Past a certain point, how could his parents know exactly what to do with him? It wasn't as though they'd had any experience with someone *like* him before. No one had.

So it seemed to Oliver that his parents were taking a guess at what was best for him, and had decided that his friends were tolerable, at least for now. Oliver wondered if that would change. He figured it had to, eventually, but tonight he wasn't worrying about it any more than he worried about most things.

They reached the kitchen to find Bane hunched over his breakfast and Phlox staring at the plasma screen above the counter. She was holding a bowl of whipping cream, a whisk poised above it. "Did you see this?" she asked.

"What?" Sebastian shuffled to the far counter, picking up an iron pitcher and filling the empty goblet waiting beside it.

Oliver saw images of the zoo from the previous night, awash in police lights, and he immediately turned his gaze to Bane, but his brother simply sat there sipping his coffee and staring into the center of the kitchen island. Oliver sat down beside him, in front of a plate that held a tarantula in suspension. He picked up the deep-fried, chocolate-dipped creature and bit off a leg, watching the news report.

Karma Kayne appeared on the screen. "It has been almost twenty-four hours since the boy's tragic death, and police and zoo staff still haven't located the missing jaguar. We've been asked to advise all residents in the area to stay indoors this evening and keep your pets in the house. If you do have to be out and about, stick to well-lit areas and make plenty of noise."

Sebastian sipped from his goblet, then turned to Oliver. "Did you see any of this when you were there last night?"

Oliver felt a wave of nerves. He sensed Bane flashing a glance at him, but he didn't meet it. "Um, we saw something going on, so we took off."

"Weren't you there, too, Charles?" Phlox asked.

"Nah," Bane replied and immediately took a huge bite from the abdomen of his spider breakfast.

"The boy died of blood loss, from a bite to the shoulder and neck," Karma continued. "The big question on everyone's mind tonight is how this dangerous cat got free. Well, police now say that this deadly event may have been caused by the *cadáveres* gang."

"Oh my," said Phlox.

Humans thought the cadáveres were simply one of the most dangerous gangs in the city, but actually, the gang didn't exist. It was a code word for passing news about vampire activity that affected the human world.

"That's unfortunate," said Sebastian.

Oliver watched the footage of the penguin enclosure from the night before.

"Stupid kids," Bane muttered with a perfect sigh. "Having their little fun, pretending to have demons and nahualli. What a bunch of maggots. Then they go and mess it up for the rest of us." He belched lightly, then slurped his coffee.

Oliver glanced at his brother, almost impressed. A trace of the bone-white paint still remained on the side of his neck, below his ear.

I don't know that he was involved, Oliver reminded himself. It was entirely possible that Bane had put the jaguar away and someone else had come along and used it to commit the murder. But then why was Bane lying and saying he hadn't been there at all? Maybe he figured that if he admitted to occupying the jaguar at one point in the evening, he'd have to answer a million annoying questions, and he didn't want to deal.

"Police are asking for anyone to come forward who might have information on last night's deadly events," said Karma.

Oliver thought about mentioning Bane's presence at the zoo. It would be nice to watch him squirm. But Oliver didn't want to be the little brother who tattled. Talk about being a lamb. And Bane would never let him forget such an offense.

"All right," Phlox announced, turning toward the boys. "Here we are." She slid two plates onto the island. "This should ease the pain of starting school again." Each plate held a fluffy Belgian waffle topped with blood-soaked strawberries, dark chocolate shavings, real maple syrup, and a mountain of whipped cream.

"Nice," said Bane, still innocent.

"Thanks, Mom," Oliver added. He dug into his waffle.

Moments later, Bane pushed back from the island. "I'm out," he announced, and headed for the stairs. As he passed, Oliver prepared for the usual punch to the back, or hard slap to the head, but neither came.

"Charles, you can wait for Oliver," Phlox instructed.

"The lamb is old enough to walk to school on his own already, Mom." Bane continued right out of the kitchen.

"Charles!" Phlox called after him. Oliver watched her glance at Sebastian, who only raised his eyebrows.

In the past, Phlox would not have stood for Bane's disrespect. She'd likely have lunged after him and delivered a tongue lashing, but now she only sighed with resignation. "Well then. Obviously you'll be fine, Oliver. I just like the idea of you two heading to school together like kids, but I suppose that time has passed."

"It's okay," said Oliver. He felt in his pocket, where he had Bane's necklace. Amazingly, Oliver felt a sliver of guilt at having it, and had thought about giving it back to Bane on their way to school. Now that opportunity was gone, and Oliver also reminded himself that any sympathetic feeling for Bane was dumb. *If he found something of mine,* Oliver thought, *he'd probably smash it right in front of me.* Besides, Oliver wanted to know what it was for, and Bane would never tell him.

"Good luck with your first night of school," said Sebastian as he trudged down the hall toward his office.

"Thanks." Oliver ate slowly, then grabbed his sweatshirt, and, with a heave of his shoulders, headed off to face the inevitable start of another school year.

✸

Far too soon, Oliver found himself walking around to the back of the looming brick school building. Fresh chalk drawings from the humans' first day were being erased from the pavement by a light drizzle.

A gaggle of slightly younger students was entering, so Oliver hung back until he could go in alone. He knocked and Rodrigo, the vampire night janitor, opened the door.

"Welcome back, Mr. Nocturne, sir."

"Hey, Rodrigo," said Oliver. He stepped inside and headed up the wide staircase. All the neon, spray-painted grotesqua had been redone for the new year. It covered the humans' happy back-to-school bulletin boards with demonic faces and moving scenes of battle.

Oliver looked back at Rodrigo, who was standing silently by the door. "It looks great," he said.

Rodrigo looked up with a start. "Oh. Oh, thank you, sir." Rodrigo did all of the grotesqua himself, changing it faithfully for each new school year and holiday. He nodded at Oliver with a wide grin, and Oliver wondered if he was the first kid to bother complimenting Rodrigo on his artistry.

He walked alone between groups of students who were milling in mellow clusters, saving the usual wall climbing and horseplay for later school days. Oliver heard mutterings here and there about the jaguar killing.

When he entered his classroom, he found an alarming change. In the past, the boys would have been congregating on one wall of the candle-lit room and the girls on the other. But now, there was a mixed group of boys and girls in a circle on the ceiling, upside down on their knees, the girls giggling and the boys joking all loud.

Oliver saw Theo with Kym leaning on his shoulder. Suzyn, Maggots, and Theo's other friend Jesper were up there, too. Oliver had heard that Theo and Kym had started going out over the summer. Theo even left a warm fox's heart on Kym's sewer doorstep, which was pretty serious. As a result, all the other boys and girls were flirting to keep up. Just now, Maggots mumbled something and punched Suzyn, then pretended not to have done anything.

"Don't . . . touch me," Suzyn muttered, scowling and rolling her eyes. Maggots tried to laugh in response, but once no one was looking, his face soured to a disappointed frown.

"There's Nocturne," Oliver heard Theo murmur to Kym. The group grew quiet, leering down at him in unison. Oliver crossed the room, head down, as whispers rippled above.

"He's such a freak!" Theo suddenly blurted in his three-times-too-loud way. Others in the group snickered.

The other half of the class was scattered around the corners of the room, either alone or in pairs, all trying to look as if they were just fine with what they were doing, and yet every now and then glancing up at the

< 58 >

ceiling crowd. Oliver passed Berthold Welch, who was making the world's smallest spray-paint grotesqua design on the wall in the corner.

"Hey, Berthold," Oliver said. He didn't usually say "Hi" to Berthold, not because Berthold was kind of an outcast — really, he was probably much higher on the popularity ladder than Oliver these days — but just because Oliver didn't usually think to say "Hi" to most people.

"Hey, Oliver," Berthold squeaked in reply, hunching his shoulders to block Oliver's view of his tiny art.

"Hi, Oliver," whispered Carly, a lone girl by the windows, as he trudged by. She was looking wistfully out into the night, stroking a tiny white mouse with her thumb. As Oliver passed, he heard a crack and then a light sucking sound as Carly had her breakfast.

He slid into his chair and found Seth already seated beside him, listening to headphones. Oliver saw Seth glance up, and so he offered a little nod. Seth frowned, looked to the ceiling to see if they were being observed, then murmured, "What's up?"

Theo laughed loudly again. Oliver forced himself not to gaze at the ceiling group. He didn't even want to be up there, and yet, it was a struggle to keep from checking to see what they were doing.

"How was the rest of your summer?" Oliver asked Seth. He sort of thought of Seth as a friend. Seth's mom,

Francyne, worked for Half-Light as the Central Council liaison, and so she and Phlox had become friends, although Oliver wasn't sure if they'd seen each other all summer. Francyne did have a new baby daughter, but that should have meant that Phlox visited more instead of less.

Seth rolled his eyes and pulled off one of his headphones. "Fine."

Oliver noted Seth's tone. "Is it still not cool to talk to me?"

Seth's face contorted. "I don't know." He lowered his voice. "Look, everyone just wants to know what's going on with you Nocturnes."

"What's that mean?"

"I don't know, like, my mom was talking about how your dad screwed up some big prophecy thing . . ."

"Oh." Oliver felt a burst of nerves. "You know about the prophecy?"

"Everybody knows now," said Seth. "Well, not *them*." His eyebrows indicated the ceiling. "But they never know anything." He smiled for a moment, then it faded. "Everybody at Half-Light knows, though."

"Right . . . Well, um," Oliver began, "my dad tried, but in the end, things worked out with the Artifact —"

"Yeah, but then, like, your brother messed things up, too."

"Well, yeah —"

"And then there's you and your *human*. I mean, it's like, if I had your destiny, I'd be —"

"Not screwing it up?" Oliver finished.

"Pretty much," Seth agreed.

"Well, it's not that easy," said Oliver. "I . . . I'm not *trying* to screw it up." Oliver stopped there, though, because the truth was that he hadn't tried to screw it up *yet*.

"My mom wants to know why another family wasn't chosen for it. I mean, it's an honor, you know."

"Huh," Oliver replied. An honor? That was how everyone saw what he considered to be more like a curse.

"Guh!" Suddenly Maggots crashed to the floor, breaking a desk in two.

"Don't," Suzyn hissed from the ceiling, "ever try that again."

The ceiling gang exploded into laughter.

Oliver reclined in his chair, preparing for the endless night, but as his knee scraped against the underside of his desk, he heard a sound like crinkling paper. He sat up and felt beneath the desk, checking in with his senses as he did so. There was a familiar scent, and now he found a note wedged into the bars underneath.

The paper was peach colored with green lines, folded carefully into a rectangle. A long diagonal fold stretched across its front, and a tiny point of paper stuck out from this, with the word "pull" written on it. Oliver did, and unfolded the page. On it was rounded writing in glittery red. Oliver immediately slid the note back beneath the shadow of his desktop, and read:

hey O – sooo bored ... tree bark bored ... first day back and it's math math math with a side of who cares ... but guess what? 1 bet you already figured it out with your creepy nose – this is my seat this year! my classroom, my seat. well technically it was Melina's seat, but then Ms. Davis suddenly had the urge to switch her with me ... 1 wonder why she had that thought? tee ... hee ... w.b.s. super nose. and don't forget about Saturday night ... – e

Oliver felt a burst of excitement, but tried to keep it off his face as he concentrated on folding the note carefully back into its rectangle shape before he stuffed it in his pocket. Emalie sat right here? And would every day? Which meant that he would find her scent lingering every night, and possibly a note, or a forgotten item . . . oh boy.

"Students," Mr. VanWick barked as he strolled into the room. He glanced at the ceiling and frowned, seeming to immediately understand how his class had changed over the summer. "Untangle yourselves, please, and take your seats. I'll expect you to focus whatever brainpower you can spare on your studies." The students groaned as they dropped to the floor.

"We have a new textbook for this fall," Mr. VanWick continued. "Seth and Carly will pass them out."

"Smelly minions," Theo chided from his seat. One of the leather-bound textbooks darted across the room and smacked him in the face.

"You can have yours first, Theopolis," Mr. VanWick commented dryly, to a chorus of hissing chuckles. "Now, books to chapter one, 'Great Successes in Cannibalism,' and we'll begin."

Oliver found, as Mr. VanWick began his gravel-toned lecture, that with the note from Emalie fresh in his mind, he had barely any brainpower left over.

CHAPTER 4

A Familiar Customer

Oliver trudged home after school, exhausted, his now cruelly heavy backpack straining his shoulders. All he could imagine was a handful of gummified tapeworms and a few levels of Night of the Developer 3 to wash away the long school night.

"Oliver."

He looked up to find Phlox striding down the sidewalk toward him, wrapped in a long black coat, hurrying like she did when there was a lot on her mind.

"Hey," said Oliver.

Phlox stopped. "How was your first night?"

"Fine."

"I'm on my way to Harvey's to pick up a few things for dinner. . . . Want to come?"

Oliver shrugged. "Not really."

Phlox threw an arm around him anyway. "Come on, let Mom buy you a mocha or something."

< 64 >

Oliver just wanted to go home, and almost wriggled free of his mom's arm. But a mocha sounded kinda good, and more important, this would give him a chance to ask Phlox something that had been on his mind all night. "All right," he said.

They weaved through quiet neighborhood streets, asleep except for the cats and raccoons. The fact that Phlox was even taking the surface streets was new this summer. In the past, she'd have preferred the sewers, except on the coldest, dreariest nights, which she loved to walk in. Now, they used the streets almost everywhere they went.

Oliver had once asked: *Why are we going this way?* and Phlox had replied: *The fresh air is good for our skin.* This was technically true, although the vampires kept their sewer tunnels warm and dry as well. But Oliver had accepted his mother's lame explanation because he knew the real reason that they weren't using the tunnels: Phlox was avoiding other vampires, and their judgment. Like what Seth had said. The Nocturnes didn't just have Oliver, the problem child, anymore. Now they were the problem *family.*

"So," said Phlox, "a new school year."

"Pretty much," Oliver grunted.

"Are the kids still making fun of you about your human friend?" Oliver felt a stab of frustration, noting how Phlox didn't use Emalie's name, even though she obviously knew it. But whatever, at least she wasn't angry about Emalie anymore, even if, like Sebastian, she didn't exactly sound happy about her either.

"A little," Oliver replied.

"And have you seen Bane this evening?"

"Not in the twenty minutes since school."

Phlox was quiet for a moment, and when she spoke again, Oliver understood why she'd wanted him to come along to Harvey's. "Has he seemed . . . okay to you lately?"

That was a funny question. When did Bane ever seem okay? But Oliver could tell that Phlox was worried. He wondered if she suspected Bane's involvement, or at least presence, at the zoo. "Not really," Oliver answered honestly. "He's been more of a jerk than usual."

Oliver expected a scolding word in response, but Phlox only sighed. "You'd tell us, wouldn't you, Ollie, if you knew that he was up to something dangerous? Even if he asked you to keep it to yourself?"

Oliver almost laughed. "Why would he ever tell me anything?"

Phlox smiled, yet it didn't douse the worry in her eyes. "Well, he's certainly been mute around us." She left it at that.

Oliver thought again about the zoo murder. Should he mention something now? But what? He didn't know anything more about whether Bane had been involved, and the more time went by, the less likely it seemed. And anything he said would lead Phlox back to Bane, and Bane, along with his annoying fists, back to Oliver.

Besides, they were nearing Harvey's, and Oliver had *his* question to ask. It had been on his mind since he'd talked to Seth. He tried to remember back to how Emalie had helped him talk to his dad at Hades' Well. She'd found the right questions to ask, the right way to ask them. Oliver wished she were here now, but she wasn't so he just blurted it out: "Why us?"

"What's that?" Phlox replied, though Oliver was pretty sure that she'd heard him.

"Why us, Mom? Like, why do I have to be the prophecy kid? Or why did you and Dad have to be the parents of the prophecy kid? I mean, why not some other family?" Oliver had been going over this in his head all night. The prophecy said that a demonless vampire child would come along, but it didn't say when, or who. Half-Light had decided to take matters into their own hands and create one. So, why had Phlox and Sebastian been chosen by Half-Light?

Phlox didn't answer for a moment. Ahead, a possum lumbered across the street.

"Well," she said finally, "we applied."

"Applied?"

"Yes." Phlox spoke slowly, like she was choosing her words carefully. "Half-Light asked for applicants from within their associate and senior staff. Sebastian was just barely high enough up the ladder. The procedure was special, and your father and I thought it might be our only shot at having a child."

This was the first that Oliver had heard of any of this. "But you'd had Bane."

"Oh, well . . ." Phlox said uncertainly. "Yes, of course, but this was after that. We wanted another child and we were having trouble. . . ." She trailed off, again seeming to think hard about what to say next. "Anyway, Half-Light picked us and we started the force treatments to prepare for siring you. And it worked."

"Huh," said Oliver. It sounded fairly normal, a little boring even.

Phlox shrugged. "There was no other way to have you, Oliver." She reached over and rubbed his back. "I know you had no choice in the matter, but here you are, and the responsibilities of the prophecy are worth it, to me."

"All right." Oliver found that he kind of liked the thought of his parents trying so hard to have him. *Yeah, great, so they get to have their kid, only I have to destroy the world.* Still, it did help a little.

They emerged from sleepy houses and reached a busy intersection. In front of them was a gas station and convenience store called 24-7. Above the pumps, which were busy with cars, was a giant, glowing sign advertising the current, comically high gas prices, which had the humans in a panic. They were so silly sometimes. The vampires had stopped using oil and gas for energy decades ago.

Atop the sign was a tiny square marker displaying a red neon circle with a black plus sign in the middle. This symbol let the vampires know that this 24-7 was also their local Harvey's Discount Sanguinarium and Confectionery.

Oliver and Phlox crossed the street and entered the starkly lit store. Aside from occasionally hurrying in to pay for gas or buy cigarettes, humans rarely ventured inside. They couldn't help feeling like there was a friendlier place somewhere else, a place that was, well, warmer. There were only a few vampires in the store at the moment, and Oliver figured that Phlox was glad to see this.

The place looked like any other twenty-four-hour convenience store. Its shelves were stuffed with unhealthy, overpriced snacks, and too-small packages of kitchen and bathroom necessities. Its walls were lined with refrigerators, featuring row after row of sodas, juices, teas, soda-juices, juice-teas. . . . The wall behind the counter was devoted entirely to cigarettes and scratch tickets.

< 69 >

Oliver walked beside Phlox as she took a basket and proceeded down the first aisle. She stopped in front of the piles of bag snacks, reached carefully between the Doritos, and pulled the very last bag from the back of the shelf. It looked like Doritos, except for a tiny Skrit symbol hidden on the bottom corner of the package. A human would have been surprised to open this bag, because it was full of blood-fried, spicy-hot triangles of alligator skin.

Phlox put the bag in her basket, then carefully rearranged the bags on the shelf into neat, equal rows, her lips clicking as she counted to herself. Oliver had counted the bags, too: twenty-five bags now in perfect rows of five. This order gave him a satisfied feeling.

They continued to the line of refrigerators. "Grab some Coke," Phlox instructed. Oliver did so, and rejoined his mom at the display of sport drinks. Phlox ran her hand under the fourth shelf from the bottom. It passed under a small blue light, which scanned her and verified that she was a vampire. There was a click, followed by a quiet humming. The shelves began to move apart vertically, and rows of hanging blood bags slid forward in the new spaces.

The bags were clear, vacuum sealed, and marked with black labels covered in white writing. Each row contained blood from a different animal. For some creatures, there was more than one style to choose from, like pig, where there was the standard swine variety or the more expensive free-range organic. There was even blood from pigs whose diet included poison dart frogs, whose toxins were great for teeth whiteness and bacterial protection. This was the variety Phlox preferred.

"Anything you're in the mood for?" she asked.

"Panda maybe," Oliver replied.

Phlox selected a few bags, then ran her hand under the light again. The bags slid out of sight, and the sport drinks returned to their usual position.

She moved to the refrigerator case of beer and cocktail drinks. A similar switch made the shelves morph, only this time the bags that slid forward were marked with silver writing. These were filled with human blood. Again, there were varieties that affected price: age of the victim, lifestyle, or specialty additives like cayenne, cocoa, or various venoms.

"Oliver, can you get some tapeworms?" Phlox asked. She continued shopping, topping off her basket with fine white flour, unrefined sugar, pure maple syrup, and a few tarantulas in suspension, which were hidden in the ice cream freezer.

"Sure." Oliver drifted away, pausing as he passed the magazine racks. A vampire man was carefully pulling a copy of *Bloodlust* from its hidden location behind *Newsweek*. Oliver knelt and reached for a copy of *Teen Fang!* On the cover was Tryshia Twilight, flashing her fangs like she was the underworld's greatest thing. Oliver didn't care much for her, or any of the teen stars, but sometimes the articles about bands were good.

He moved to the aisle of candy snacks, most of them made of disgusting artificial sweeteners and colors — humans really were so deprived — and reached back through the rack of Twizzlers packages. He selected the last package, which was actually full of gummified tapeworms. Again, you had to know where to look on the label. He was counting and rearranging the bags when he felt a presence nearby, like someone was watching him.

"Those have all the protein that a growing boy needs."

Oliver looked up across the tops of pretzel bags to find large, pale lavender eyes peering at him beneath bright magenta hair.

Lythia LeRoux.

Oliver tried to keep the surprise off his face.

"Oh," Lythia murmured, leaning forward with a hand beside her mouth as if she were talking about someone else. "He's shocked to see me."

Oliver thought he should reply — *Say something, anything!* — but as seemed to happen around Lythia, he couldn't decide what he should say and so ended up standing there like he was broken.

Lythia plucked a can of tuna from the shelf and added it to the shopping basket that hung from her elbow. Oliver noticed human blood and a bag of frozen Gila monster heads in the basket, but also strange objects like a steak, two more cans of tuna, a box of baking soda, and a bundle of fresh datura root.

"Poor Oliver," Lythia said, sucking air through her teeth. "Still having trouble with comebacks, I see."

"No. I —" Part of Oliver's problem was that he was trying to think past what Lythia was saying and figure out what she might *really* be up to. She had a habit of saying one thing and being up to something else, like at the roulette table in Tartarus, when she'd talked with Oliver and Dean as if they were complete strangers, even though the whole time she'd been Dean's master.

Oliver also had trouble around Lythia because she had an intense presence: Though she looked about Oliver's age, she had a demon. Not only that, he'd seen her perform complicated adult vampire skills such as Evanescence, which even most vampires Bane's age couldn't do. It was like she was some kind of prodigy. Combine that with her piercing lavender eyes and the way she talked to him like she always knew something he didn't, and all Oliver could manage to do was stammer like an idiot.

In Morosia, Lythia had been after Selene's summoning charm, and she'd used Dean to get it. Her father,

Malcolm, was a key member of Half-Light, but in Italy, Emalie had sensed that Lythia was up to something on her own. Strangely, if it hadn't been for Bane, who stole the summoning charm from Dean before he could deliver it, Lythia might have succeeded in whatever it was that she was really up to.

This time, well, Lythia's eyes were still just as arresting — *Stop it!* Oliver shouted at himself — but what was she doing here in Seattle?

Lythia made a show of touching her finger to her chin pensively. "How about if Oliver says: Oh hi, Lythia, so lovely to see you!"

"Why would I say that?" Oliver managed to reply.

"Ha, obviously because you *do* think it's lovely to see me — don't you?" Lythia smiled, baring her perfect teeth. She'd applied glitter polish to them, a popular style among vampire girls, and so her teeth sparkled with flecks of gold. "Or he could say . . ." Lythia began speaking in a high-pitched child's voice. "No, Lythia, please don't kill my human girlfriend!"

Oliver froze. "What —"

"Leave her alone! She's my special little blood bag!"

Oliver's arm thrust forward. As soon as he realized what he was doing, he knew it was a mistake, but he had already hurled the bag of tapeworms at Lythia. Her face didn't even twitch, and her hand shot up and caught the bag. Then she burst into a snickering laugh.

"Watch out for big bad Oliver!" she taunted. "Nice to see you, too, though I would have preferred a kiss." Lythia smiled wickedly. "It would be the least you could do."

Oliver felt battered by each thing she said. *Say something witty!* he thought desperately. *Stop standing there like an idiot!* It was horrible.

"Don't worry, Oliver, I know it's hard to use your words," Lythia continued as if Oliver were a toddler. "I'm a busy girl these days anyway, what with controlling your minion friend and plotting to save you."

"What do you mean *save me?*" he groaned.

"Lythia to the rescue!" She grinned. "Don't worry, you'll find out when the time is right. Poor thing, that's how it always is for you, isn't it? Never a clue what's going to happen next."

Her hand flashed out, and the tapeworm bag hurtled back and smacked Oliver in the face, his hand arriving a second too late to deflect it. He stumbled backward.

Then Lythia was being raised off the ground, an actual note of surprise on her face. "What —"

A black misty presence had wrapped around her and she was lifted two feet into the air. It looked like a girl, wrapped in veils.

"You don't always have a clue what'll happen next, either," whispered Jenette in her ear. She dropped Lythia and raced to Oliver's shoulder. "Hi, Oliver," she said, her voice reverting to its mousy whisper.

"Um, hey," Oliver replied.

Lythia staggered to keep her balance, a look of disgust on her face. "So this is your thing, eh, Oliver? Having little girls come to your rescue?" She glared at Jenette. "I'll come for you, too, smoky."

"Please, please do," Jenette hissed.

"Oliver?" Phlox was walking down the aisle, peering at Lythia. They'd never met, and Oliver could see Phlox trying to figure out who Lythia was.

"And Mommy, too!" Lythia clapped. "Oliver, you *are* the ultimate ladies' man."

Oliver once again searched his suddenly empty brain for a response. There had to be something he could say that wouldn't make him sound as lame as he looked. Something that would let Lythia know that she couldn't mess with him and his friends.

But once again, the moment passed.

"Well, Oliver, just wanted to say hi," Lythia purred. "See you around, 'kay?" She turned to Phlox, smiled sweetly, and then dashed down the aisle and out the door without paying for her items.

Oliver watched her go, shaking his head. He was pathetic. "Thanks," he muttered to Jenette.

"No problem," said Jenette. "She's hideous."

"That and a lot of other things," said Oliver grimly.

"Was that Lythia LeRoux?" Phlox asked, arriving beside him.

"Yeah," Oliver replied.

"Last I knew, Malcolm was on business in Naraka." Phlox sounded concerned. "Did she say anything to you about what she's doing here?"

"Nothing that made sense."

"I'm surprised that he'd be in town without Sebastian knowing," Phlox said, then frowned. "Maybe I shouldn't be." She looked at Oliver. "Have you noticed any thing . . . strange with Dean?"

"No," said Oliver, but he worried. If Lythia was around, she could make Dean do whatever she wanted. *Or maybe she's been giving him orders all summer,* Oliver thought, *and I just don't know it.* This was going to be a problem.

"Well then, come on, Oliver. Let's get going," said Phlox, her concerns returning to the possibility of running into other vampires. She started toward the door.

"Where were you guys last night?" Jenette asked, sounding hurt. "I waited at the graveyard till dawn."

"Ahh, sorry," Oliver said. As a wraith, Jenette was helpful in the cemeteries when they were searching for Oliver's parents. She could float among the graves and determine in moments whether any of the bodies had similar force signatures to Oliver's. He didn't really understand how she did it. "We got sidetracked . . ." Oliver didn't want to say any more with his mom around. "We'll meet you there Saturday night, okay?"

"Well, I'm not sure I can get away from The Shoals again Saturday," Jenette pouted. "It's not that easy, you know."

Oliver nodded. Jenette was controlled by a powerful Merchynt demon named Spira, who inhabited the borderlands and sold wraiths for special jobs. Oliver didn't know much about Jenette's world, but really, she seemed to be able to get away whenever she wanted. "Can you try? We need you. And I promise we'll be there."

"Swear it to me." Jenette curled around so that her smoky, veiled face was inches from Oliver's.

"Um . . ." Oliver stepped to the side, but Jenette stayed face-to-face. "Right, I swear."

"Then I'll be there," Jenette said. She sounded very happy.

"Oliver." Phlox had reached the door.

"See you then," said Oliver, and he turned to leave, his mind on Lythia and what she might be up to.

CHAPTER 5

A Disturbing Absence

As Oliver dressed for school Thursday evening, he found Emalie's note in his pocket. He knelt and dug into one of the drawers beneath his coffin. His fingers found a cool ivory box, and he grasped it carefully with two hands before removing it. The jewelry box, in which he kept the trinkets he'd collected from Emalie, was so full at this point that it would barely close. He'd even ripped out the inner padded lining to make extra space.

As he opened it, the tiny toy television that she had used as a locating charm in Italy fell into his lap. Oliver placed it back among the earring, other notes, and hair bands, then added the latest note. Just this sliver of paper made the box that much harder to close. It looked like a half-open clamshell. He was going to need something larger.

Across the crypt, on the other side of Bane's coffin, a black table stood along the stone wall. Oliver eyed a disorderly pile of boxes atop it. They were from Phlox's birthday back in July. The pile had been moved down here from the living room after the party. The fact that Phlox had not immediately organized the boxes and stored them in their proper places — and had now let a *month* go by — was further evidence that his parents were not themselves these days.

Under the guise of being helpful, Oliver started organizing the pile, folding up the materials that vampires reused over and over to give gifts: satin wrapping, horse mane ribbons, and wooden boxes that collapsed on hinged sides.

What he was really after, though, was a maroon wood box with gold etchings of dragonlike Pyreth demons: creatures from the lower worlds that inhabited the borderlands, like the caverns around The Yomi. They were fiercely territorial, and so were often used as symbolic guardians. This box was the perfect size to hold Oliver's ever-growing Emalie collection.

As he turned, he was overwhelmed by a noxious odor. He saw that Bane's coffin was slightly ajar. Phlox had told Bane it was his responsibility to sift his own sleeping soil, and it had clearly been months since Bane had done so. That pungent bacterial smell, mixed with the lethal aroma of Bane's new cologne, was hideous and yet, strong as the smell was, Oliver's sensitive nose could tell that it was old. Bane hadn't come home since breakfast the other night.

Oliver headed upstairs and was just entering the kitchen when Karma's voice caught his ear.

"This second attack took place in the early morning hours . . ."

Phlox was watching the screen over a mug of coffee.

"The victim was out delivering newspapers with his father."

A disheveled, tearstained man appeared. "He ran around to the side of the building, that's where the mailboxes are, and I heard a scream . . ."

"Police are doubling their efforts to find the killer animal."

"Have you seen your brother lately?" Phlox asked, peering at Oliver.

"Not since yesterday," said Oliver truthfully.

Phlox shook her head. "Well, I suppose he'll get around to coming home sooner or later. I know I shouldn't worry about him."

"Our sources indicate that the investigation has not ruled out the possibility of further involvement by the cadáveres gang."

Sebastian entered the kitchen, shaking his head. "Sounds like it's definitely a vampire."

"Did Half-Light call?" Phlox asked.

"Tsss," Sebastian hissed, scowling. "I don't know who they've got on the case, but it's clearly not me." He gave his regrowing arm a sour glance.

"That's fine with me," said Phlox. "I'd be even more fine if Charles would come home."

Oliver saw the tight lines on Phlox's face and felt a tightness in his own gut. Another attack, coinciding with Bane being gone. *But why should I care?* Oliver thought, annoyed. If Bane was involved in the killings, that was his problem, not Oliver's. Except that it kind of was. Oliver thought about what Seth had said, how Phlox avoided the sewers, and even how Half-Light wasn't calling Sebastian to help with this crisis. If Bane was behind this, he was only going to screw things up even more for the whole family.

Yeah, but if I was in this kind of trouble, would Bane even take a second to worry about me? Probably not, though he had tried to help Oliver last winter. Bane had wanted to *fix* Oliver by having him kill a human. Of course, Bane's actions had given Lythia the opportunity to turn Dean into a zombie, but still — he couldn't use his brother as a standard for how to act. After all, they were very different.

"Guys," Oliver said carefully. "I don't know if it's important but —" Phlox and Sebastian both turned to him. "Bane *was* at the zoo the other night. When I saw him, he was Occupying the jaguar."

Sebastian's brow darkened. Phlox's eyes started to glow. "Why didn't you tell us this sooner?" she asked tersely.

"Well, I didn't really think Bane did it, I mean —"

"It's all right," said Sebastian, "We don't know anything, and it's probably not Charles." He looked at Phlox. "I'll have to report this to Half-Light."

"Don't be ridiculous," Phlox snapped. "We can't report this to Half-Light or Central Council. If they think it's Charles, given the trouble he's been in lately, they might —" Her eyes glowed more fiercely.

"Phlox, this isn't that serious."

"Yet." Phlox slapped her mug onto the counter and paced across the room. "We can't even ask the other families to keep an eye out. With how they think of us, word will get right back to Half-Light."

"Well, then we'll find him ourselves," said Sebastian.

Phlox nodded. "You should get to school, Ollie," she said. "Thank you for telling us."

"Can't I help you look for him?" If nothing else, it sounded better than a long night at school.

"Let us handle it," said Sebastian. "I'm sure he'll turn up soon enough. These two things probably aren't even related."

Nice try, Dad, Oliver thought. For an attorney, he didn't sound very convincing.

Oliver headed to school, lost in worried thought. He was glad he'd told his parents, but their reaction, especially Phlox's, only made his sliver of worry about Bane grow. She'd referred to the trouble he'd been in lately — stealing the summoning charm, missing school . . . or was there more? If it turned out that he was the jaguar killer, would the punishment be more severe for him because of that?

Oliver found himself hoping for the first time that his brother would turn up, but he didn't that night, or the next.

✱

Saturday evening, Oliver leaped off the back of a city bus and walked up the steep hill to the front of Emalie's house. He sat on the bottom step and waited in the crisp darkness, his thoughts on his family. There hadn't been another jaguar attack in the last two nights, but the animal was still missing, and even more troubling, so was Bane. Phlox and Sebastian had been out almost nonstop looking for him. Oliver still had a hard time imagining that Bane was really behind the jaguar killings, but then again, why else wouldn't he be coming home?

Oliver was pulled out of his thoughts by shuffling footsteps. "'Sup," said Dean, sitting beside him. "How was the first week?"

"Whatever," said Oliver.

"Did your brother show up yet?"

"Nope." Oliver turned and studied Dean's blotchy face, remembering now that there was a whole separate problem to deal with.

"What?" Dean asked.

"Nothing, it's just — I saw Lythia. Have you seen her?"

Dean instinctively glanced around. "No, wait, you mean here, in town?"

"I saw her at Harvey's." Oliver explained the encounter. Even as he did, he worried. What if Dean was under Lythia's orders right now? There was no way to be sure.

Something scraped above them. Oliver looked up to see Emalie leaning out her upstairs window and reaching to the eave of the roof, where a thick rope was coiled around a hook. They had affixed the rope so that Emalie could sneak out without having to creep through the rest of her house. The rope dropped to the ground. It had thick knots in it to help her climb. Emalie swung out and shimmied down, landing with a grunt.

Oliver watched her blow a loose strand of hair from her eyes, thought it was cute, realized he was staring, panicked, and tried to look somewhere else casually.

"Hey, guys," Emalie said, smiling. Then she saw their worried faces. "What?"

"Lythia is in town," Dean said. "Oliver saw her."

Oliver recounted the story again.

"Great," Emalie grumbled. "Dean," she said carefully, "have you — um —"

"No," Dean groaned, "nothing!" He glanced from Emalie to Oliver. "Stop looking at me like that! I had no idea she was here, I swear."

"Okay," Oliver said, but inside, his trust of Dean crumbled with each thought. *Lythia could be telling him to say that*. Oliver rubbed at his jaw where Dean had broken it under Lythia's command. This was not good.

"Do you think there's a way to block her orders?" Emalie wondered aloud. "You know, make it so Dean can resist her?"

"I don't know," said Oliver. "Maybe. I could check the library."

"Désirée might know," Emalie added.

"Mmm," Oliver murmured and frowned. The last time he'd seen Dead Désirée she had given him clues for how to talk to Selene, except she'd done it in such a way that Oliver hadn't understood what she'd meant until it was almost too late. Would it have been so hard for Désirée to say: *Oliver, go talk to Selene, the oracle that gave your prophecy, and oh, by the way, she's hiding in fireflies*?

But with Désirée it was never that simple. And visits to her shop were always uncomfortable. Oliver couldn't help wanting to avoid it.

And yet, now there were three reasons to go see her: Dean, Oliver's questions, and — Oliver felt in his pocket, his fingers touching the smooth glass of the pendant on Bane's necklace. He pulled it out. "I could ask her about this, too."

"No luck figuring out what it is?" asked Dean.

"No," said Oliver. "I looked in a Skrit dictionary at school and did a search online. But it didn't show up." The more time Bane was mysteriously gone, the more Oliver was curious as to whether the necklace held a key to what he was up to. It was probably time to tell his parents about this, too.

"How are *you* feeling?" Dean asked Emalie.

"Ah, I'm all right." She yawned. "Just a little tired. It's a lot harder being nocturnal now that school's started." Oliver knew that Dean had been referring to the way she'd passed out the other night, but Emalie didn't bite. "I have a new math teacher, and I don't know if it's going to be a guaranteed nap this year like it used to be. But whatever, I'll make it work."

She started down the stairs to the street. "Hey, I heard there was another jaguar attack."

"Yeah," said Oliver.

"Do you think it's Bane?" Emalie asked carefully.

"I don't know."

You're worried about him, aren't you?

Oliver's eyes snapped to Emalie. She'd spoken in his head, and now gave him an embarrassed smile. Oliver remembered back to Italy: Emalie had said that only the little television charm could invite her into his head — but he'd been suspicious that she could get in whenever she wanted.

Sorry, Emalie said guiltily.

"Right," Oliver said aloud, his voice suddenly hoarse.

"What?" Dean asked, his gaze flashing between them.

"Nothing," Emalie replied.

"Ugh." Dean rolled his eyes.

The roar of the bus reached their ears, but instead of stepping up beside the bus stop shelter, the three shrank back into the shadows. The bus squealed to the stop and let off passengers. Just as it was lurching away from the curb, Oliver and Dean each hooked an arm with Emalie.

"Ready?" Oliver asked. They rushed forward and leaped, soaring up and landing atop the departing bus. They sat down in a row, legs stretched out, leaning back on their hands, the moist breeze massaging their faces.

"I love these seats," said Emalie.

"So," said Dean brightly, "where to tonight?"

Emalie pulled out their graveyard map and unfolded it. "We were going over to Capitol Hill the other night, so, same place? It's in the second circle, but not too far out."

Emalie was referring to circles they'd drawn on the map with a red marker. The circles were centered on the address from Oliver's human parents' obituary. The first circle had a mile radius from where they'd lived. The second was two miles and so on, until the circles were too big to fit on the page. They'd been able to search some cemeteries online and had crossed those off the list. Now they were concentrating on the ones that were left.

"Yeah, that's a good one to check," Dean said. "I read that it's got a bunch of residents from that time period."

As Oliver listened to Dean, he thought: *He could be leading us into a trap. This could be Lythia's doing.* What was he going to do about these thoughts?

"Okay, same place," Oliver agreed slowly. "I told Jenette we'd meet her there, since we stood her up the other night."

"It's not like it was a *date* or anything," Emalie grumbled.

"No," Oliver said carefully, "but it's hard for her to get away from The Shoals."

"Well, maybe she shouldn't come as often as she does," Emalie continued.

Oliver glanced at Dean, who shrugged his eyebrows.

The bus was rumbling to a stop at a traffic light. Ahead, the road crossed a freeway overpass.

It's just kind of annoying, Emalie pouted in Oliver's head, *how Jenette totally likes you, and acts all —you know.*

Um. Everything suddenly felt hot and claustrophobic in Oliver's head. Did she hear *everything* he thought? Then he remembered back to just moments before, when she had dropped down from her window and Oliver had thought how cute she looked — *Oh no, I just thought about thinking about it! She might have heard that, too!*

Oliver glanced nervously at Emalie — was that a smile twitching at the corner of her mouth? Her dark eyes were focused right on him. *Guh,* Oliver thought nauseously. He looked away again. *Think about something else!*

Dean started to stand. "Time to transfer," he announced. Another bus was turning left in front of theirs, heading for the on-ramp to the freeway. "Let's go."

They hooked arms again and vaulted into the air, arcing high over the traffic and landing on the next bus as it rolled onto the freeway.

They took their rooftop seats once more. Oliver untangled his arm from Emalie's as quickly as he could, then resumed trying not to think about anything that he wouldn't want Emalie to hear — but what about what she'd already heard? How often was she in his head?

It's really not that often, I swear.

Bah! Oliver wanted to jump, to flee. "Just, don't,"

he spat and immediately hated how annoyed it had sounded.

Emalie's face fell. "Fine."

"No, I don't mean, it's just —" Oliver felt like he was falling down a staircase. Each possible thing he could say was like a hard marble step slapping against his shins, his stomach, his head. Why couldn't he just — *talk*!

"Everything okay?" Dean asked, glancing from one to the other.

"Fine," Emalie said, pouting.

The bus crossed a high bridge over a ship canal. Below, long docks jutted out into the water, lined with floating homes. Their lights twinkled on the water. To the right, the gasworks loomed over Lake Union. The buildings of downtown blinked in the darkness.

The bus veered off an exit ramp and slowed, continuing on a road that paralleled the highway as it ran alongside Capitol Hill. Steep layers of apartments and houses rose above the far side of the freeway. On the other side, similar layers of homes dropped down to the lake. The highway rose slightly beside them, and now the dark underbelly of the overpass was visible. Oliver was busy looking away from Emalie, not really paying attention to what he saw —

When he spied the pale white apparition again.

CHAPTER 6

The Third Attack

It was floating in the dark beneath the highway, weaving among cement pylons. Oliver could see its willowy form more clearly — blurred lines sketching out a human form, edged with silver and electric blue.

"Hey, do you guys see that?" Oliver pointed, but right when he did, the apparition slowed, no longer keeping pace as the bus followed a curve in the road and passed under the highway.

"What?" asked Dean.

Oliver twisted around. The apparition was lost among the shadows, but Oliver found a very certain thought in his head: *It's waiting for me.* "We need to get off," he said, and jumped to his feet.

"Wait, why?" Dean asked. "What did you see?"

"Come on, Dean," said Emalie knowingly.

They hooked arms and leaped off the bus, stumbling in an awkward landing on the uneven dirt. Oliver peered around the gloomy world of pylons and shadows. Above, the heavy concrete structure roared and shivered.

"It's cool in here," said Emalie, pulling her old camera from inside her jacket. She twisted the focus, composing a shot, but then lowered the lens, her eyes wide. "There it is," she whispered.

Oliver followed her gaze and saw the apparition ahead. It was hovering by a long staircase that zigzagged down from Capitol Hill, under the highway, all the way to the lake.

"And what exactly is that?" asked Dean, peering ahead.

"Not sure," Oliver replied. "An apparition, I think. I saw it the other night, at the zoo." He started toward it.

"Wait." Dean grabbed his arm. "Is it dangerous?"

"I don't think so," Oliver said and kept walking. Again, he felt a sense that this thing wanted to communicate with him.

The three moved closer. The apparition remained in place. As Oliver neared the staircase, he could see the faintest lines of a face, of hair.

"We're right near your human parents' old house," Dean said absently. "For whatever that's worth."

Oliver barely heard him. He was within twenty feet

of it now, close enough to hear the faint hissing sound of its sparking edges. Then the apparition started to move, floating up the staircase. Oliver reached the stairs and turned to follow it — when a familiar animal scent reached his nose.

"Oliver!" Dean whispered, smelling it, too.

The concrete stairs rose to a landing that was surrounded by tangles of blackberry bushes. There sat the jaguar.

"Um . . ." said Emalie.

The apparition floated by the cat, up the stairs and out of sight.

The jaguar hissed at them, then turned and slinked back to the next set of stairs — and stopped, turning back to eye them before it kept going.

Bane? Oliver thought.

"I think it wants us to follow it," said Emalie.

"Wouldn't that be kind of dumb?" asked Dean reasonably.

"Come on," said Emalie, starting after it.

"Emalie, wait!" Dean called.

"No, she's right," said Oliver, falling into step behind her. In fact, he wasn't sure that she was, but he wanted to see the apparition again.

They climbed to the first landing and found the jaguar perched atop the next set of steps, silhouetted by a sidewalk lamp. The apparition was halfway up the steps behind it, continuing to float up and out of sight. In the light, Oliver could make out an eeire orange glow in the jaguar's eyes. And there was another scent on the air up here — of death.

"Uh-oh," Dean commented.

The cat turned and padded away up the next steep staircase, almost like it was following the apparition. The trio climbed after it and found themselves in a paved alley between brick apartment buildings. There were large Dumpsters here and there against the walls, with lines of trash cans between them. Oliver's eyes darted from the trash to the iron fire escapes above, his nose checking for the jaguar and also for the source of the ominous scent.

They reached the street. There were more apartment buildings in both directions and a small playground across the road. Oliver spied the jaguar sitting expectantly at the edge of the park grass. It purred, turned, and disappeared behind a wooden playground structure.

"And we're sure we're not about to get eaten?" Dean wondered as they crossed the street.

"Never sure of anything," said Oliver. "Just a feeling."

"I don't think it wants to eat us," Emalie said, sounding confident. Oliver wasn't feeling certain of the jaguar's intentions at all, so why was Emalie? But he did feel like the apparition wanted them to see something. Something that had to do with the animal. Only the apparition was nowhere to be seen.

They reached the climbing structure and stopped beside a metal slide. Swings dangled empty nearby, their seats covered in dew.

"Doesn't this have 'trap' written all over it?" Dean asked.

"It's —"

Thwump!

A body landed on the slide.

"Ah!" Emalie cried, a sound Oliver had never heard her make.

It was a girl's body, her lifeless eyes gazing up into the night. Oliver looked up to see the jaguar standing atop the peaked roof of the play structure. It hissed again.

Emalie was staring at the body, transfixed. "Do you hear anything?" Oliver asked.

Emalie nodded. "Her name was Jamila," she said softly.

Oliver knelt beside the body, glancing warily at the jaguar, up on its perch. He reached gingerly to the girl's neck and pushed her black hair out of the way. "She hasn't been dead very long," said Oliver. "A few minutes, maybe." He saw the large wounds where the jaguar's teeth had done their work — and there between the gashes were two puncture holes, clearly made by vampire teeth.

The scent of the human blood momentarily overwhelmed him. Oliver felt woozy, and a strong urge overcame him — *Take a bite.*

"Oh." Oliver turned to see Emalie frowning at him.

"Sorry," said Oliver quickly. "I didn't —"

Emalie shook her head. "Forget it," she muttered, yet avoided his eyes.

Oliver felt a burst of frustration. How could he constantly guard his thoughts against what Emalie might hear while so much else was going on? It was starting to drive him crazy.

He glared at the jaguar above. "Bane! Is that you?"

"It's him," Emalie whispered. Her eyes were closed and she was holding her ruby scarab, its chain dangling around her neck. It was a conduit charm. By placing it between her hands and blowing on it, she could travel into minds.

The jaguar hissed viciously.

"Emalie," Oliver began worriedly. The last time he'd seen her try this, with Lythia, she'd ended up getting hurt.

"Bane's in there," Emalie reported, "but he's not in control. Something is holding him prisoner." She winced.

"He can't stop the killing. . . . and he thinks it's . . . because of . . . Nnnnaa —" She suddenly slumped over, her eyes rolling back, her lips quivering.

"Emalie!" Dean rushed over and grabbed her by the shoulders.

"What —" Oliver began.

"Oliver, watch out!" Dean shouted as he pulled Emalie away.

Oliver whirled.

The jaguar leaped off the roof, hurtling through the air and landing on Oliver, crushing him to the ground. Its eyes blazed orange, its jaws were inches from his face, its putrid breath blasting him with the smell of blood. There also seemed to be a strange, bitter spice odor: Was it datura? This felt much more dangerous than when Bane had been playing around the other night in the park.

"Get off him!" Dean plowed into the cat with his shoulder. They tumbled onto the grass. Oliver jumped to his feet. The jaguar righted itself and slashed at Dean, raking his face with thick claws. "Geh!" Dean crumpled to the ground.

"Stop it, Bane!" Oliver screamed, his eyes igniting in amber.

The jaguar hissed at him, ears flattened against its head, then turned and fled, bounding into the street. In a moment it was lost in the shadows between cars and buildings.

"Dean — "

"I'm fine," Dean groaned, standing up. When he turned, he didn't look fine. Four long gashes extended down the side of his face. He felt at the wounds. "That's gonna leave a mark," he muttered, then reached down for a handful of sand, which he began rubbing into the black, bloodless wounds, to keep them from getting infected.

"Where's Emalie?"

"Over here." Dean led Oliver across the street, behind a car. Emalie was lying against the trunk of a large tree, eyes closed.

"Yrr fall . . ." she mumbled quietly.

Oliver leaned close to her. "What, Emalie?"

Her eyes fluttered open . . . and looked shockingly different. Her irises had turned bloodred, her pupils white. Her hands shot up and grabbed Oliver by the throat. "*It's your fault they're destroying me!*" she shouted, her voice edged with a demonic hiss.

"What's she talking about?" Dean asked frantically.

Emalie's grip was so tight, Oliver couldn't take in a breath to speak. If he'd been a human, she'd be choking the life out of him.

"Emalie, knock if off." Dean reached down and

yanked her hands away, tearing Oliver's shirt in the process.

"Don't touch me!" Emalie screamed. She got her feet beneath her and lunged away with more than a human's speed. She landed like a cat, eyes still smoldering, pupils white hot. "You don't —"

A bewildered frown crossed her face, and just like that, her eyes returned to normal. Emalie rubbed at her head. "Sorry . . ." she mumbled, then looked around. "W . . . What happened?"

"Lots," said Dean.

"Emalie," Oliver said carefully, rubbing at his neck, "something's going on with you."

Emalie shrugged, then started looking around with concern. "Where's Bane?"

"He took off, still in the jaguar, he —" But Oliver stopped, hearing a familiar sound. "Sshh."

A bat circled in the air above the playground. It swept low by the body, and a swirl of black smoke grew from it. Tyrus McKnight, Sebastian's partner at Half-Light, appeared. He wore his long black coat and high turtleneck sweater. He bent toward the girl, pushing up his small round glasses as his narrow nose did the same detective work that Oliver had done.

The blackberry bushes rustled at the edge of the park, and a raccoon appeared, black smoke rising from it as well.

"How's it look?" asked Tyrus's partner Leah. She had dark skin, frizzy hair, and dark red eyes.

"Like an Occupied jaguar," said Tyrus.

He produced a glass ball from his coat and popped it open. Using a small black stick, he scraped a bit of blood from the girl's neck and wiped it into the sphere. He clicked it closed and stood, pulling out a square black gadget with a depression in the middle. He dropped the ball into this, where it spun and hummed.

Tyrus read from a blue screen. "It's him again. Malcolm will be pleased. His little Nagual is working nicely." Tyrus pocketed the device and turned to Leah. "Safe to call our intrepid detective?"

Leah closed her eyes, held out her hands, and swirled her palms. The air rippled like liquid around them. "The animal is almost a mile off — wait — someone else is here."

"Come on!" Oliver hissed. They sprinted for the alley.

"Where?" Tyrus asked in the distance.

Oliver, Dean, and Emalie bounded down the lengths of stairs until they were back under the highway. They ducked behind a pylon and watched the staircase and the skies, but no one seemed to be in pursuit.

In the distance, a police siren warbled to life.

"Bane's in a bad way," said Emalie.

< 101 >

Oliver studied her exhausted face. "That was Bane talking through you up there, wasn't it?"

Emalie's brow furrowed, like she was searching her thoughts.

"Like he did in Italy," Dean chimed in.

"It . . . yeah." Emalie nodded. "It was."

"He said, *'It's your fault they're destroying me.'* Did he mean *my* fault?" Oliver asked.

Emalie shrugged.

"Who's destroying him?" Dean asked.

"I don't know," said Oliver. "I don't know of any enemies that Bane has."

"Tyrus said something about a Nagual," said Dean. "What's that?"

"Don't know that either," Oliver replied.

"Whatever it is, Bane can't escape it," said Emalie. "And he's scared."

"Bane?" said Oliver incredulously. "That's hard to imagine." Oliver couldn't remember ever seeing his brother scared.

"He is," said Emalie. "I can tell." Oliver was surprised to hear worry in her voice.

"So, I don't get it," said Dean. "If Half-Light knows there's a vampire in the jaguar, then why are they telling good ol' Detective Pederson? Wouldn't they want to hide the mess and solve it themselves?"

"It doesn't make sense," Oliver agreed.

More sirens wailed in the night.

"Now what?" asked Dean.

"There's still time to hit that cemetery before Jenette gets too upset." Oliver glanced to Emalie, but she had no smart quip, just more of the same vacant gaze.

"That's okay," a mousy voice whispered from nearby, and Jenette swirled between them. "I got bored waiting and came to find you."

"Oh, hey, sorry, we —" Oliver began.

"Don't worry. I heard what you were saying. I sensed that body up there, too. Not good."

"Yeah, well . . . We should go," said Oliver. "It's not far to the cemetery, right?"

"Yes, master," Dean mumbled absently.

Oliver glanced at him worriedly. "What?"

"Huh?" said Dean. "Oh, nothing."

"We don't need to go," said Jenette. "Your parents aren't there. I checked while I was waiting. It doesn't take me long."

"You're sure?" Emalie asked.

"Of course I'm sure," Jenette replied. "I passed through every pile of bones in that place, and there was no connection to Oliver. If his parents were there, I would have known."

"I still don't get how you can sense them," said Emalie doubtfully. "They've been dead for almost fifty years. Their spirits would be long gone."

"Well," said Jenette, her tone getting a touch defensive, "there are more forces than just spirits. And with all that Oliver's told me about his parents, it will be pretty easy for me to feel the concentration of forces that they'd have."

"What do you mean, all the things I've told you?" Oliver asked. "We've never talked about my parents. I . . . I don't remember anything about them."

"Oh . . . right," Jenette stammered quickly, "Well, I . . . I don't mean what you *actually* said, I mean what your emotions tell me. You really know a lot about them, Oliver, inside."

"Great. Somebody else who's in my head," Oliver muttered.

"What?" Emalie and Jenette both asked at once.

"Nothing! It's just that I don't feel like I know my human parents at all."

Jenette smiled. "You do. Trust me."

"Hey, guys." They turned to Dean, who had taken a few steps back. His face looked strange, his eyes darting about. Behind him, a bus was approaching the underpass.

"What is it?" Emalie asked.

"I . . . have to go . . ."

"Dean, what's up?" Oliver asked nervously.

Dean frowned further. "Oh man . . . I think I'm being . . . summoned."

Oliver understood in a cold flash. "By your master."

Dean managed a regretful face. "See ya," he began, and then as if someone else was pulling the strings, his mouth stretched into a thin grin. "Suckers," he spat, and Oliver could hear Lythia in Dean's voice. Then Dean turned and vaulted into the air, landing atop the bus as it passed by him.

"We need to stop him," Emalie said, starting toward the road.

Oliver held her back. "No. Let him go. There's nothing we can do." He watched the bus roar away and cursed to himself. This was terrible! Dean could never be trusted if this could happen. And Lythia could do whatever she wanted. Oliver wondered sadly if he could even hang out with Dean anymore.

Please don't give up on him.

"Uh!" Oliver shouted and spun to Emalie. Here was that feeling again, of being totally out of control. One friend was a pawn of their enemy, another was saying they'd talked about things they'd never talked about, and the other was sneaking around in his head whenever she wanted!

I'm not sneaking! Emalie thought. *I can't really help it, it's just —*

"Stop doing that," Oliver snapped. He hated the coldness of his voice, but he couldn't take it anymore. This was all just too much.

"Fine," Emalie spat. "I won't help."

"That's not what I mean."

"Emalie," Jenette said, "Oliver needs privacy in his head."

"Oh, you're one to talk about people's heads being private!" Emalie shouted. "But it was different when you possessed me!" She stormed off toward the street.

"Hey, where are you going?" Oliver called.

Emalie fiddled in her bag, then turned around. "Whatever," she muttered. Oliver saw her rolling something in her hand. It looked like a small felt bag. Then she flashed out of sight, using the enchantment that made her invisible to vampires.

"Emalie, come on," Oliver groaned.

"She's just walking down the road," Jenette reported. "I can still see her. Want me to go get her?"

Oliver shook his head. "No. Just forget it."

"Okay," said Jenette. "Sorry about that," she added, though she didn't seem too bothered by the others leaving. "Hey, wanna go down to the Underground or something? Or maybe over to the Egyptian? The midnight movie is *Time Bandits*. I love that —"

"No, I . . . I'm just gonna head home," said Oliver.

"Oh," said Jenette disappointedly.

"Sorry. I'll see you at our next cemetery, okay?"

Jenette gave a big sigh. "I guess, but I'll see you before then. I always do."

Oliver scowled at her. "What's that supposed to mean?"

"Oh, sorry. That's right, you're all paranoid now." Jenette chuckled. "Nothing, I didn't mean anything. Just playing around. Good night, Oliver."

Jenette slithered off into the dark. Oliver waited, leaning on a pylon until the next bus arrived. Between troubled thoughts about Bane, Dean, and now even Emalie, he glanced around for any sign of the apparition. He found that he really wanted to see it again, but it didn't appear.

When he returned home, he found the house strangely empty. His parents were still out, and there was no sign that Bane had returned.

CHAPTER 7

A Plot Revealed

After one of his most sleepless days in months, Oliver dragged himself out of his coffin early the next evening to find the crypt empty. The kitchen was as it had been when he'd returned home: startlingly messy, dishes and goblets from many days of hurried meals piled carelessly. Oliver began organizing and counting them without thinking about it. Once they were arranged in neat, orderly stacks, he turned to leave, then imagined his parents out there somewhere, no doubt exhausted, and turned on the faucet.

As the hot water filled, he took a steel canister of coffee from the cabinet, the Eternal Dark Roast with cayenne pepper. He scooped some into the grinder, then transferred the grounds to the coffeemaker. He filled the carafe from a tiny tap on the side of the sink. The Nocturne home was secretly connected to the human water system, but any water for drinking was first run through a special filter to add a touch of

< 108 >

bleach, which helped with whitening teeth and killing bacteria.

Oliver poured the water into the machine, spilling a bit as he did so. He grabbed a towel to wipe it up. He'd rarely been the one in the house to make the coffee, and while it felt kind of important to be in charge of it, the circumstances undermined the feeling.

Once the pot was steaming and gurgling away, Oliver set to scrubbing the dishes, and his mind quickly returned to the night before, to Emalie storming off, and to Dean being summoned.

Dean. Oliver couldn't shake the memory of him speaking like Lythia and dashing off to do her bidding. Maybe he'd been doing it all along. What if he'd been reporting to her about everything Oliver did? He might not even know he was doing it. What if she could simply read Dean's thoughts whenever she pleased? And most important, what was Lythia really up to?

Thinking about it gave Oliver that overwhelmed, crowded feeling in his head. All his thoughts seemed to be fighting for space and yelling for his attention at the same time.

The coffeepot beeped. Oliver filled a stone mug, the brown one that his father often used, then slugged back the coffee while it was still nice and scalding hot. His tongue and throat exploded in flames from the cayenne.

He finished the dishes, refilled his mug, got himself a plate of leftover Sepulcrit casserole from the fridge, and ate alone at the kitchen island. He paused at every faint sound of rats upstairs or neighbors in the sewers, hoping it might be either his parents or his brother.

When he was done, he threw on his sweatshirt, made sure Bane's necklace was in his pocket, and headed downtown, determined to get some answers.

He used the sewers. Traffic was light, and when he passed other vampires, Oliver just kept his gaze straight ahead. As he walked, he took some slight enjoyment from the warm air, mellow candlelight, and that faint smell of time wafting off the ancient art on the walls. It was nice to be down here again.

He emerged from a manhole behind the Seattle Public Library. Celia St. Croix greeted him at the back entrance, and he proceeded into the empty human library, where he took the number two elevator down to the lowest listed floor.

The door slid open at the concrete parking garage, and Oliver performed the counting password: "One," he said to himself, then pressed the P button again. "One, two." He pressed it again. "One, two, three, four," and a third time. The elevator's chime rang three times, the doors slid closed, and the elevator lowered toward a floor unmarked and unknown to humans.

The doors opened into the quiet, plush vampire library. The Librarian, a wiry old man in a fine suit, greeted him warmly. "Good evening, Mr. Nocturne. Right this way."

Even though the long room, with its deep burgundy carpet and mahogany walls, was almost empty this early in the evening, the Librarian still followed the custom of leading Oliver to one of the lamp-lit tables along the wall. "Let me know if I can be of assistance," he said politely, and departed.

Oliver twisted the silver gooseneck lamp toward him and spoke quietly into the copper microphone at its end. "Blocking a zombie's master." There was a moment of silence, during which Oliver glanced up and found the Librarian gazing at him curiously. That always bugged him, but he was getting more used to interested stares these days.

"Forty-one," the pleasant female voice of the Catalogue replied.

"Nagual demon," said Oliver.

"Ninety-three," said the Catalogue.

Oliver turned to leave the table when he had another idea. He turned back and said: "Prophecy reversal."

The Catalogue was silent.

"Proph —" Oliver began again, but the Catalogue replied:

"That topic is not currently contained in any known

Tome. Please refer to the Central Council for further information."

"Thanks," Oliver said, not surprised. He turned and proceeded to the end of the room and through heavy black velvet curtains. He entered the stacks, a series of floors made of grated metal, with hallways of curtained chambers, each holding an ancient vampire called a Codex.

Codex forty-one was located two floors below where Oliver was standing. He wound down a spiral staircase, then proceeded down an aisle, past black curtains with numbers engraved in plaques beside them. He stopped before the curtains for forty-one. "Enter," instructed the Catalogue from a hidden speaker above.

Oliver ducked into the dark chamber and took his seat on the single pillow in the center of the room. Tendrils of incense smoke lingered in the air. Single candles on each wall cast spare light.

"Blocking a zombie's master," said Oliver.

Two glowing emerald eyes lit in the dark, and a pedestal slowly rolled forward with a grinding of gears. The Codex, wrapped in hooded crimson robes, inhaled deeply, its breath rattling with difficulty as the ancient vampire began to speak.

"The zombie is forever linked to the master. There is no way to undo the bond without destroying the zombie."

"What about slaying the master?" Oliver asked.

"With the master slain, the zombie will return to the earth."

Oliver sighed. So much for that idea.

"It is possible, however, for the connection between a zombie and its master to be temporarily blocked," the Codex added.

"Explain."

The Codex breathed in deeply. "A master's influence over a zombie may be interrupted by the placing of a *hindrian* enchantment upon the zombie. It does not break the connection, but rather makes the connection difficult to find for a time, thus blocking unwanted visitors from the mind."

A question popped into Oliver's head. "Can it be used against an Orani?"

"Its documented uses do include Orani deterrence."

"How is it done?" Oliver asked.

"There is an ancient Skrit. When correctly etched into a channeling mineral, such as magnetite, it may then be prepared and activated with the life force of a transcendent one."

Oliver didn't quite recognize that term. "A transcendent one?"

"A being who has achieved awareness above his or her known world."

"For example?"

"Most common is an oracle."

Oliver started. Could that be . . . "Show me the Skrit."

The Codex raised a hand, and yellow smoke wavered before him. In it, a Skrit appeared in red outline.

Oliver pulled Bane's necklace from his pocket to be sure. The symbols were exactly the same.

"How is it prepared?" Oliver asked.

"Using coyote musk and aniseed," the Codex replied.

"Thank you," said Oliver, standing and bowing. He left the Codex chamber and walked back through the stacks, his mind racing. Bane had a hindrian enchantment. When he'd had Selene's summoning charm, he could have obtained a drop of her life force. But she'd been strong. Sebastian had attacked her with a mystical stiletto and she'd still escaped.

Maybe she gave it to him willingly. But why? Why would Selene help Bane, and not only that, why did he even need the enchantment? *Because he was worried that someone would hear his thoughts. Or that someone might try to get inside his head.* That meant Bane had been up to something that he wanted to keep secret. But from whom?

This all still fit with Oliver's original suspicion about why Bane had stolen Selene's summoning charm: that he was jealous, that he wanted to be the chosen vampire, and maybe even that he was trying to find a way to get Oliver's prophecy for his own. He could have used the enchantment to keep his plans secret. But it didn't make sense that Selene would help him with that.

Oliver felt another wave of frustration. If Bane had found a way to transfer the prophecy to himself, he could have just asked, for all Oliver cared. Really, he would have been happy to give Bane the prophecy and be done with it. *Except then Bane would go through with it, and my friends would be destroyed.* That was why Oliver had to keep it and find a way to undo it himself. But how? The Codex had no information on that. Maybe Désirée would.

He arrived at chamber ninety-three and entered. He sat and said: "Nagual demon."

Pink eyes lit and the Codex rolled forward. It took a rattling breath. "Nagual are vampires who have been consumed by their animal nahualli. Nagual were first documented during the Aztec and Mayan empires. Some vampire shamans experimented with feeding datura root to their nahualli animal, which was thought to create a deeper bond between the vampire and the animal's spirit. But the balance was hard to get right, and the animal spirit was seductive in its primitive simplicity.

"Sometimes a vampire would go too far, and lose itself *within* the animal. The vampire's physical body would be permanently lost. This new creature was called a Nagual — part *vampyr* demon, part animal spirit — and could leap from one animal to the next.

"In recent centuries," the Codex continued, "Nagual have been trapped and sold on the black market. While vicious, they can be controlled by certain totems and made to obey commands. Nagual are especially useful for lethal tasks, as they are cunning and powerful."

Oliver could barely absorb what he was hearing. His brain felt too full, but then his thoughts began to organize and suddenly fell into place. A Nagual could be bought and controlled. Tyrus had referred to *Malcolm's Nagual*. Half-Light had bought the Nagual, they knew it was inside the jaguar, and —

Of course. They *knew* it was Bane. They were *trying* to get him into trouble. Oliver could hardly believe it, but it made perfect sense. If Bane was trying to somehow steal the prophecy, who else to protect Oliver other than Half-Light? They would have been watching Bane since Morosia, trying to figure out what he was up to. But Bane had the necklace, which kept his thoughts safe. Once it was lost, though, Half-Light could learn what he was up to. And whatever it was, it must have been bad enough that Half-Light felt they needed to trap him in the jaguar and frame him for the murders.

That would give them an excuse to . . . what? Punish

him, Oliver guessed, maybe even lock him away somewhere.

It's your fault they're destroying me, Bane had said. Did he mean that Half-Light was framing Bane to protect Oliver and his prophecy? If so, then didn't Bane know that he deserved it? *And why would Selene help him? Why would the jaguar and the apparition have led us to that body?*

Something about this didn't add up, didn't feel right. As much as Oliver had imagined his brother's jealousy and spite, he just couldn't believe that Bane would really have been plotting something *so* bad for his own brother that Half-Light thought it was in their best interest to frame him. Especially since Half-Light's best interests often weren't the same as those of Oliver and his family.

"Defeating a Nagual demon," said Oliver to the Codex. He needed to hear Bane's side of this *from* Bane. It was the only way to know for sure what was going on. And he'd have to get Bane out of that jaguar to do it.

The Codex began: "The Nagual can be —" suddenly it was cut off by the pleasant Catalogue from above:

"I'm sorry, this topic has been deemed classified. Please refer further queries to the Central Council."

"Thanks," Oliver grunted, and left the chamber. Of course, Half-Light had taken care to remove any information that would endanger their plan. *Désirée would know how to defeat it,* he thought. But he didn't want to go to Désirée's alone. He needed to round up his friends.

But instead, Oliver found himself heading home. First, he wanted to tell his parents what he knew. Dean couldn't be trusted, and Emalie — well, she might need another night to cool off. *Stupid,* Oliver scolded himself. He didn't need to snap at her like he had, but he just couldn't help it.

"Guys?" Oliver called as he entered the house, but there was no answer. Oliver considered going to look for them, but they could be anywhere. It was probably best to stay here until they returned. They *had* to come home at some point. He hoped it would be soon.

Oliver sat on the couch and lost himself in a video game. He played and played, but his parents still didn't come back. Eventually he dozed off where he sat.

❈

Oliver awoke to the sound of footsteps. He got up and walked into the kitchen. Phlox and Sebastian appeared, looking exhausted. "Hey, guys, I —"

But they weren't alone.

"Hello, Oliver."

Tyrus entered behind them, followed by Leah.

"Come on, Oliver," said Phlox gruffly, passing him.

Oliver followed them into the living room. Phlox and Sebastian slouched onto the couch. Their faces were blank, their eyes heavy with exhaustion.

"Have a seat," said Tyrus. He and Leah stood in the center of the room, coats on.

Oliver glanced at his parents. Phlox nodded. He slid into a deep chair.

"Oliver," Tyrus began. "I've just been explaining to your parents —" He took off his glasses, pulled a handkerchief from his coat pocket, and rubbed at the lenses. He almost looked nervous. *He doesn't want to be doing this,* Oliver thought. "Your brother has gotten himself into quite an unfortunate situation."

Oliver looked over to see his father watching Tyrus darkly. Phlox was staring at the floor, picking at her fingernail. Oliver's first instinct was to reply *I know,* but now he doubted whether that was a good idea. Maybe it was best not to let Half-Light know what he knew.

"I'm sure you've heard about the recent jaguar killings," Tyrus continued.

"Oh. Yeah," Oliver said innocently.

"Well, I'm afraid it's your brother who's been Occupying the jaguar."

"Wow," Oliver mumbled, trying to sound stunned.

"Obviously this is complicated," Leah continued. "It's become a serious situation. We're using all of our available resources to find him, but so far, our search has proved difficult. We're very worried that Bane will kill again."

"What's going to happen when you find him?" Oliver asked.

Phlox's fingernails clicked sharply, tearing at one another.

"Well," Tyrus spoke slowly. "Unfortunately, it's the decision of Central Council, and they feel that, due to the uproar this is causing in the human community, it has become a serious threat to the balance of our existence. A breach of our code on this magnitude must be punished harshly in order to send the right message to our kind."

"Just get to it," Phlox growled.

Tyrus looked at her awkwardly as he continued. "Bane will need to be confined and assessed. If he can be rehabilitated, we'll do everything in our power. If not . . . well, I'm afraid you know that answer."

"Dust," Phlox whispered.

"What?" Oliver couldn't help himself. *Slay* Bane? But had he really been up to something so serious that he needed to be dealt with in this way?

"Sometimes a vampire is beyond repair," Leah said matter-of-factly. "And the community needs to know that we take this kind of offense seriously."

"But," Oliver began, unable to help himself, "but that's not —"

"Oliver." He found Phlox glaring at him. "Not now."

"But Mom, they —"

Phlox's eyes flared. "I said *not . . . now.*"

Oliver sensed that Phlox was not scolding him, but rather making a pact. "Fine," he muttered.

He couldn't believe this. Slaying a young vampire was a big deal, and would no doubt cause outrage in the community — unless there was a good reason, like a series of murders. And Oliver remembered what Tyrus had said to his parents before the trip to Morosia: *The prophecy must be put above any one individual.*

"You still haven't explained what this 'assessment' will be, Tyrus," said Sebastian.

"Seb, you know the drill. It's not just the rule-breaking, or even the incident in Morosia. Three killings in such rapid succession? There's the question of his bloodlust at this point. He may be beyond help."

Phlox hissed quietly, her eyes glowing faintly. "So, that's it, then?"

"Look, Phlox, you know I don't like telling you this," said Tyrus. "Everybody feels terrible about it."

"Of course they do," Phlox snapped.

"Mr. Ravonovich wants you to know," said Leah,

"that Half-Light will do everything in its power to help Bane once we find him."

"Will we even be able to see him?" Phlox asked quietly.

"Of course —" Tyrus began.

"Assuming there's not a struggle to apprehend him," said Leah, her tone matter-of-fact.

"Oh, that would be so convenient, wouldn't it?" Phlox spat.

"We'll obviously do everything in our power to avoid that end," said Tyrus.

Phlox smiled thinly. "And so we're just supposed to accept this."

Tyrus nodded soberly. "I'm afraid there's no other way."

Oliver saw Phlox grasp Sebastian's hand.

"Thanks for coming by," Sebastian said, business-like. "And I suppose if I ask to help you in finding Bane, you'll tell me that I can't with my arm in this condition."

"You'd be a liability," said Leah.

"Another happy coincidence," muttered Phlox.

Tyrus shrugged. "What can I say?"

"I think you've said plenty," Phlox hissed.

"Tyrus, we should go," Leah said, motioning toward the door.

Tyrus glanced from Sebastian to Phlox, and seemed to be searching for something else to say.

"We get it, Tyrus," said Sebastian. "Be in touch when you know more."

Tyrus and Leah quietly left.

Oliver sat. His parents sat. Minutes ticked by.

Finally, Phlox looked over to Oliver. "Go get ready for school, and you can tell us on the way," she said, and stood purposefully.

CHAPTER 8

Outbursts

Oliver met his parents on the street outside their house. In his long coat, Sebastian almost looked like his old self, except for the sleeve pushed above the regrowth chamber.

Phlox had tied her hair back severely, and wore a long leather coat. "We're going out to look for Charles again," she said, and started off.

"Is that where you've been the last few days?" Oliver asked.

"Well, you don't think we were waiting around for the magic word from Half-Light, do you?" Phlox muttered.

"Phlox," cautioned Sebastian. "Yes, we've been searching."

They walked up the street in a light rain.

"Oliver, whatever it is you've found out," said Phlox, "I didn't want you to say it in front of them."

They passed under the Aurora Bridge, by the stone statue of the troll.

"They were lying to you," said Oliver.

"We figured as much," said Sebastian.

"I . . . I ran into Bane Saturday night."

"You did?" Phlox asked anxiously. "What was he doing?"

"He was in the jaguar, and had made the kill," Oliver explained. "But Emalie said that he seemed trapped inside it — not in control. Bane took off, then Tyrus and Leah showed up. They checked the body to make sure Bane had done it, and then they called Detective Pederson."

Phlox and Sebastian stopped, turning to Oliver.

"What?" hissed Phlox.

"They said that Malcolm LeRoux would be pleased to see that his Nagual was working."

"Y —" Phlox began, but stopped. She turned a fierce gaze toward Sebastian. "They're setting him up."

His eyes met hers, then he glanced away. "So," he growled, "this is how they want to play it."

Phlox's voice grew thick. "This is our fault."

"No, Phlox." Sebastian stroked her shoulder. "It's not. I mean . . . it was always a danger with him, considering . . ."

"Don't say it," she hissed.

Sebastian gazed up into the dark lattice of metal beams beneath the bridge. He didn't speak for a moment. "Phlox," he said finally, his voice heavy, "you know the choice we made."

Oliver wasn't sure what they were talking about, and though he was hesitant to interrupt, he still needed to tell them about the necklace. "Guys —" he began.

"Sebastian!" Phlox hissed before Oliver could continue. Her eyes burned turquoise. "This is our son! We have to do something!"

"Like what?" Sebastian shouted. "Tyrus is just following orders, and Ravonovich has made up his mind. Besides, as much as you may not want to accept it, you know we agreed to all of this a long time ago —"

"You miserable kitten!" Phlox snapped. "Fine." She whirled and stalked away.

"Phlox, wait —"

"Just go home and nurse your little injury! And don't blame Half-Light for that, either!" she called over her shoulder. "I'll find Charles on my own!"

Sebastian started after her, but Phlox evanesced, collapsing into a column of smoke and sailing off on the breeze. Sebastian stopped, long coat flapping around him, his shoulders slumped dejectedly.

Oliver just stared. He hated this. Not only his parents fighting, but that he was right back where he started! Not knowing what was really going on. What were they talking about? What did Sebastian mean about a *danger* with Bane? What was the *choice* that they'd made? "Dad . . ." he began.

"Don't worry about us, Ollie," Sebastian said. "I'll find your mother, and we'll keep looking for Bane. You just go to school and have a normal night." He hurried off down the street.

"But I want to help!"

"You can't, Ollie. Just go." Sebastian turned a corner and was gone.

"Great!" Oliver shouted. He turned, kicking violently at the litter and debris along the roadside, and stalked off. Yeah, right. His dad expected him to go and have a *normal* night? Since when were any of Oliver's nights normal? And it was because of Half-Light, and Bane, and his parents, and a prophecy, and *everyone* . . . and it just totally sucked.

As he walked, his anger and confusion only bubbled hotter. Why wouldn't his parents be marching straight to Half-Light and demanding an explanation after they'd heard Oliver's account? *Because they know something I don't, again. Something about Bane.* But what? And what had they *agreed* to?

By the time he reached school, Oliver's mood had darkened to black. He found a collection of his classmates racing around on the blacktop, playing Gargoyle Tag. The game was chaotic, and played using tiny, poisonous piedra geckoes, from the underground. Usually someone brought a mesh bag of thirty or more of the two-inch-long creatures, so there were enough for everyone.

There was only one rule in the game: Everyone who had a gecko was *it*. The goal was to squash your gecko against the small of another player's back, so that its insides soaked through the other player's shirt.

When the juices of the gecko seeped into skin, they would spread up and down the spine and through the entire skeletal system, turning the player's bones to stone — which hurt a *lot* — and freezing the player for about a minute, until the toxin wore off. The player's skin would take on a stony gray color, and a demonized face would appear over the player's normal face. Tiny horns might sprout, and scales, flared reptilian nostrils, or fangs might even appear. It looked like a mild version of the *vampyr* faces that Oliver had seen in his family's portraits in Morosia. After you froze someone, you could take their gecko and use it to freeze someone else.

Oliver stopped at the edge of the game, beside Seth. "Hey, Seth," he said. Seth didn't reply, as he was currently turned to stone. His head was covered in spiky, spiraled horns, and his mouth twisted in annoyance.

The game was in full frenzy, a wild blur of excited faces and sloppy hair. The chase was intense, kids leaping high into the air to avoid one another, sometimes bounding on and off the brick school wall. For a rare moment, this school year's new social rules had been forgotten. There was Theo chasing Carly. There was Berthold sneaking up behind Kym. There was Suzyn turned to stone.

As Oliver watched his classmates, his father's words echoed in his head: *Have a normal night.* Well, here was his chance. Jump in on this game and maybe for a few minutes he could just be one of them.

But he didn't.

Why not? He wondered, annoyed at himself. *Am I just going to make myself an exile again? That only makes it worse.* He scowled at the thought. *So what? Who even cares?* None of these kids had a prophecy and all that came with it, like fighting parents, a screwed-up brother, the weight of the human *and* vampire worlds on their shoulders. What did they know?

Deep in his thoughts, Oliver barely heard the footsteps behind him in time. He whirled around to find Theo only a step away, a squirming gecko in his hand.

."Ah, so close," Theo said with a grin. "Your gargoyle face would probably be a crying little human girl."

Oliver glared at him. "You're so cool."

Theo smirked. "Nocturne, what do you know?" He darted back into the chaos of the game, bumping Oliver's shoulder as he passed.

< **129** >

Oliver watched him go, smoldering inside. Then, out of the corner of his eye, he noticed that Seth still had a gecko in his frozen hand. It writhed about, trying to get free of the stone-colored fingers.

Fine. I'll play. Oliver reached over, bending Seth's thumb back. There was a sound like crunching stone as the thumb broke, but whatever, it would heal quickly enough, and Seth wouldn't even know who did it. Oliver took the tiny, slippery lizard, held it tight, and tore off into the game.

He dodged left and right, closing in on Theo, who had spotted Kym and was sneaking up on her. Oliver was almost within in striking distance —

A large, chunky shoulder smashed into him, knocking him sideways and sending him sprawling to the pavement. Oliver looked up to see Maggots smiling down. "Gotcha," he grunted and immediately turned and slammed his shoulder into another passing person. He didn't even have a gecko with him.

Theo spun around and grinned. "Ha! Nocturne, you're hilARious!"

Oliver glared at Theo, hating him so much, but Theo just darted away after Kym, who spotted him and leaped to the school wall. Oliver's eyes burned, his insides wrapping into a knot. *Stupid!* He couldn't stand it anymore. He just wanted to . . .

Maggots was still standing a few feet away, his back to Oliver, looking for his next shouldering victim. Oliver pushed himself into a crouch, and lunged.

He hit Maggots square in his beefy back and smashed the gecko against him.

"Whu —" Maggots toppled like an old tree, rolling onto his back just in time to shade to gray and freeze, his ears sprouting out long and batlike, and his forehead growing a bony crest.

Oliver leaped down onto him. "How's it feel to get knocked around?" he shouted and punched Maggots squarely in the nose. There was a hollow crack. Oliver's hand exploded in pain, but whatever. "You like this game?" he snarled, hitting Maggots again.

"Oliver!" someone shouted, Oliver wasn't sure who, and didn't care. He thrust his fist downward again and was knocked free. He landed hard on his backside, scrambled to his feet, and was about to jump onto Maggots again, hit him again, just —

But then he saw that the entire game had stopped. All his classmates were gaping at him. It was Berthold, of all kids, who had knocked him over.

Suzyn appeared, and looked at Oliver like he was some other being entirely. "What's wrong with you?"

Oliver stared at all the glaring faces and had no reply. *What did I just do? What is wrong with me?* That was the question that never seemed to go away.

"You're going down, foot rot," Theo growled at him. "You're *so* going down."

Oliver thought he might tear apart inside. He wanted to lunge at everyone, take a swing at all of them at once. But he also wanted to apologize, to explain that he had *no idea* what had gotten into him. His brother, his parents, his destiny, take your pick! But then he still wanted to yell at them, to scream that it was their fault for being so . . . *So what?*

So normal?

"Time for class," called Rodrigo from a distance.

"Tsss," Theo hissed. He and Jesper picked up the stone Maggots by the armpits and started dragging him toward the door.

Oliver stayed rooted in place, watching everyone head inside to start the school night. He felt everything shutting down inside, almost like he was falling asleep on his feet.

As the kids crowded at the door, Oliver turned away. He vaulted over the fence and stalked off into the night.

CHAPTER 9

Enchanted Blades

Oliver headed across town. At some point, he started second-guessing his decision to skip school. *Why? Who cares about school right now?* That was the last place he could imagine being with everything that was going on.

It took him awhile to calm down, and once he did, Oliver found that he had nothing . . . no way to explain the way he'd freaked out and attacked Maggots like that. He didn't even know that he *could* act like that.

Nice one, bro. . . . Oliver imagined that, of all people, Bane would have been proud of how he'd acted moments ago. It was probably the most vampirelike thing Oliver had ever done. And it didn't feel good in any way.

Soon, he reached Emalie's house. Most of the lights were on inside, so Oliver crept carefully around to the back and peered in the kitchen window.

Emalie and her dad, Cole, were sitting at their small table, eating. Oliver could see potatoes, the roasted ones that Emalie liked to make, and pork chops. Emalie's wide eyes were fixed on her dad, who was in the middle of a story.

"And so then Zeke tripped and dumped the whole case, like — *thousands* of bait fish."

Emalie burst into laughter, her face getting red. Cole smiled and sipped his beer. He'd been working for a salmon boat fleet since the winter. Oliver had no idea what the story was about, but he knew that, not long ago, dinner between Emalie and her dad hadn't included much laughter.

Cole stood and said, "I need more of those excellent potatoes." He rubbed Emalie's shoulder and walked to the stove. He started scraping the pan with a spatula, and called back over his shoulder, "Want some, Margie?"

Emalie's face crashed.

Her dad knew it. His own face contorted. "Emalie, ah, sorry . . ."

Her eyes widened, glistening half-moons of liquid growing on their bottom rims. It took forever for the first one to fall, but once it did, it was like a dam had broken. But Emalie stayed silent, her lips pursed tight, just the clicking of her blinking, as her face drained from red to white. Watching her, Oliver wondered what crying felt like. It looked so awful, like torture.

Cole was sitting back down. "So how's school been?" he asked tentatively.

"Fine," Emalie muttered blankly, like she'd shut down inside. Oliver had seen her do this before. Dropping from the heights of happiness to the depths of sorrow. It seemed to happen more lately. Then again, the mention of her missing mom never put her in a good mood.

Oliver slipped away from the window and returned to the front of the house. Putting his hands against the wall, he felt for the forces, then scaled up to Emalie's window. She always left it slightly ajar, and he pushed it open and crawled inside, staying on the wall until he was beyond her bed. He dropped to the floor and sat against the wall beneath the collage of her photos. Most were cropped at wild angles, while a few were left in full size: the ones she was really proud of. One of them was a shot of the inside of the abandoned upstairs of Oliver's house. It showed the overturned dresser frosted in gray light through a broken window.

Emalie was still using cardboard boxes for a desk, but she had covered them with a tapestry. She still had a pillow for a desk chair.

On the ceiling, plastic stars glowed faintly. She'd been adding to her map of the constellations. In the center of the ceiling were Orion, Scorpio, and Cassiopeia, all in small yellow stars. As the map spread, the size and color of the stickers changed, but always the constellations were real ones, except for a smiley face in one corner. Oliver knew his constellations and noted Cygnus, the cross, and Ursa Major and Minor, the Big and Little Dipper. But he was surprised to see a few that he didn't recognize, directly over Emalie's bed. They were made of large, orange stickers. The shapes seemed only distantly familiar.

Light rain made a steady whispering sound on the roof. Plates clinked downstairs.

Oliver felt the calm that came over him in Emalie's room. Like he was safe. No other vampire could come here. Not his family, his schoolmates.

Soon, he heard footsteps trudging up the stairs. Oliver felt a flutter of nerves and remembered that he wasn't totally safe. He reached into his pocket, took out Bane's necklace, and slipped it around his neck. As he pushed it inside his shirt and the cold magnetite touched his skin, there was a faint tingling sensation, almost like he'd been sprayed with cool mist.

Emalie walked in, her two black cats, Amethyst and Jade, scurrying at her feet. She headed straight for her bed and threw herself on it. The cats peered at Oliver.

"Hey —" he began.

"Buh!" Emalie snapped up. She peered into the dark and didn't seem to see Oliver for a moment.

"Emalie, it's me."

"How —" she started, looking at him, confused. "But, when did you get here?"

"A while ago. I skipped school."

"Why?"

"It's Bane. Half-Light is framing him."

"Why would they do that?" Emalie asked.

"I don't know. Because of whatever he's been up to, but it's weird because they lied to my parents. They said Bane was responsible for the killings and was going to need to be apprehended and maybe slain, but they didn't say they were framing him. And then my parents said all this weird stuff about the choices they made, and the dangers with Bane . . . before they started yelling at each other. It's almost like they knew this might happen . . ." Oliver trailed off. It felt good to be saying all this out loud, but it left him feeling confused.

Emalie squinted at him. "Okay . . ." She was trying to see something in the dark.

"What?" Oliver asked.

Emalie shook her head. "Nothing." She flopped down on her back.

She just tried to read my thoughts, Oliver thought to himself, *and the necklace worked.* "I heard your dad downstairs," said Oliver quietly. "It was just a slipup."

Emalie huffed. "Yeah, well." She didn't say any more.

< 137 >

"What are those constellations above your bed?" Oliver finally asked.

"I don't know," Emalie muttered.

"Did you make them up? They're cool shapes —"

. "No, I didn't make them up," Emalie snapped, like Oliver was an idiot for thinking such a thing. "I saw them, in my head. In a dream where I was with my mom, seeing out of her eyes, or whatever those stupid dreams are supposed to mean."

"They probably mean something. You're Orani."

"Yeah, well . . . lot of good that's done."

"Anything new on your mom?"

"No. My aunt and I can't find anything on that Arcana town, from Selene's photo. I mean, there was a town, but it burned to the ground in one night. Nobody knows why, and all the records were lost. There's nothing about my mom, just like there was nothing else in Fortuna. Just like there's been nothing all along."

"What about that thing on the photo," Oliver asked, "the thing about your mom and Selene being guardians of The Muse?"

"There's, like, a million muses in history and myths and all." Emalie threw up her hands. "Who knows?"

Oliver could tell that talking about Emalie's mother was not helping. He decided not to pursue it.

Emalie kept staring at the ceiling. "Why can't I get in?" she finally asked.

"What do you mean?"

"You know what I mean," she pouted. "In your head. It's like I'm locked out."

Oliver felt a bit of guilt mixed with his relief. "I'm wearing a necklace of Bane's. It's called a hindrian enchantment. My brother was using it to keep people out of his head. I brought it to give to Dean, to help him fend off Lythia."

"But *you're* wearing it now." She sounded disappointed.

"Yeah."

After a moment, Emalie huffed again. "Did you really want to drink that dead girl's blood?"

"I — no, but well, yeah. I mean, I didn't *want* to, but it's like . . ." Oliver wondered how to explain it. Feeling the urge to drink blood was completely natural. "It's just instinct. It would be like if you smelled a hamburger and wanted to eat it."

Emalie bolted up in her bed and fixed him with a cold stare. "That's — gross."

And then she burst out laughing. "Eww," she gasped between giggles.

Oliver smiled. "It probably shouldn't be that funny to you."

Emalie laughed harder. She slid off her bed, dropping to her knees on the floor and grabbing her sides. Oliver wondered if this was normal human girl behavior. If it was, then human girls were even more mysterious than vampire girls.

Her hair brushed his leg. He almost leaped to the ceiling.

"It's like that old cartoon," she cried, "with the two guys on the boat, and they're so hungry, and one of them looks at the other and he turns into a hamburger, and the guy starts shaking salt on him." She giggled, snorting.

"Ha," Oliver tried his hardest to laugh along, yet he felt unnerved. Maybe because Emalie was being so silly about something that, in reality, wasn't. Maybe because a second ago, she'd seemed totally depressed. Or maybe because her hand now accidentally brushed against his foot. Oliver thanked the necklace once more.

Which reminded him about Bane. Oliver slid to his feet. "Want to go out?" he said.

Emalie rocked onto her knees, her laughter subsiding. "Sure." She grabbed her vest and canvas shoulder bag.

Oliver crawled down the wall. Emalie shimmied down the rope. They walked to the bus stop and waited in the shadows.

Emalie huffed lightly. "I wouldn't have to ask 'where to' if I could just check your head."

"Yeah, well." Oliver tried to brush off the comment. "We should go to Désirée's," he said seriously. "If we're going to rescue Bane, we'll have to deal with this Nagual demon, and all I know about them is they're strong."

"Wow."

Oliver glanced nervously at Emalie. "What?"

"You just sound all, like, determined. Rescue plans and everything."

"Well, I've got to at least try," said Oliver.

The bus pulled up. They linked arms and leaped onto the roof. As the bus rumbled off, they both pulled their sweatshirt hoods up against the drizzle.

"I know," Oliver continued, "that he's the same brother who's always such a jerk, but still . . . , I guess I want to help him anyway. Is that crazy?"

"No," Emalie replied.

"Besides, I don't trust Half-Light. And maybe this thing with Bane has to do with me," Oliver said. "I don't know how. Like maybe it's my fault or something."

"Oliver, not everything is your fault."

"Yeah, well. Anyway, he's my brother. Shouldn't that matter?"

"I don't know. Does it matter to vampires?"

Oliver shrugged. "I think it does to me."

"Okay," said Emalie. "But what about Dean?"

"Don't know yet, maybe go find him after Désirée's."

They jumped off the bus downtown and entered the sewers. Oliver felt Emalie's hand grip his sweatshirt lightly. He glanced back at her, but found that she had done her disappearing trick. Except with the necklace on, Oliver couldn't hear her voice.

They twisted down to the Underground Center, entering through platinum double doors. As they weaved through the milling crowds of finely dressed vampire shoppers, Oliver was jostled, and felt Emalie's hand slip away.

Where had she gone? He probably didn't need to worry about her, and yet, he pulled off the necklace and stuffed it back in his pocket.

Thanks, said Emalie a second later. *I'm a few people back, but I see you.*

Okay. Oliver's fingers closed around the necklace, ready to put it back on, but he decided to leave it in his pocket.

They reached the first gap between the platforms. Oliver stopped and waited for Emalie to put her arms around his shoulders so he could leap down to the lower floor. Instead he felt a tap on his arm.

I think I can do this with you.

What?

I don't know. When I'm invisible like this, I can sort of feel those forces that you feel. I think I can probably levitate with you. Go ahead.

But what if you —

Oliver felt invisible hands shove him, and he fell off the edge of the platform, bumping into other vampires as he did so. "Watch it!" one of them yelled.

Oliver grabbed on to the forces and righted himself. He lowered to the next level, then turned back.

Right here, said Emalie from beside him. *That was sweet.*

Nice. Oliver couldn't believe that Emalie had just, in essence, levitated. A human — and while performing an enchantment to cloud a crowd of vampire minds to her presence.

I'm getting good, right?

How are you doing that?

I just feel it. It's, like, I pull back from the world. It gets blurry around me, like I'm outside it, and then I can just kind of swim along to wherever I want. Isn't that cool?

Um, yeah. Yet as impressed as Oliver was by Emalie's growing powers, he couldn't shake the recent memories of her passing out.

You just have to be worried about something, don't you?

Oliver could hear her frown, but didn't answer. They'd reached the glass revolving door to Dead Désirée's Drug and Alchemy Emporium.

Oliver felt a familiar twinge of reluctance as they

entered Désirée's lair. It was the usual airless quiet inside, only the light Muzak playing from the ceiling, barely audible. The shop looked as white and spotless as ever, its pale lights gleaming, its shelves neatly lined with black glass bottles and wood boxes. And yet the corners, though hard to focus on, still had that slight green tinge of grime, almost like there was some darkness hidden beneath all this light.

Oliver headed down the aisle. Ahead, the high counter was vacant. As usual, there seemed to be no other customers in the store. The air smelled of bleach. Their footsteps made no sound on the tiled floor.

Oliver wondered if now he should put the necklace back on. Maybe it could help him avoid that eerie feeling of Désirée picking through his thoughts.

He turned to Emalie, but found that she was still nowhere in sight. *What are you doing?* He thought frantically.

I'm gonna see if I can fool Désirée. . . .

"Of course you can't." Oliver whirled to find Désirée standing in her spot behind the counter, smiling, her long fingers touching at the tips. Her crimson hair was tied back, her pale skin smooth, her lavender eyes peering intently from behind narrow glasses. Oliver was reminded of Lythia's eyes for a moment, especially since Désirée gave him a similar, speechless feeling.

Emalie popped back into view beside Oliver, looking embarrassedly at the floor.

"I am impressed though, Emalie." Désirée hadn't called her by name before. Emalie shuddered slightly. "Your powers are progressing rapidly. I never doubted you'd pick up on your Orani nature quickly, but there was much debate as to how you'd fare when you began your liaisons with the dead. Many bets were placed."

"Who debated?" Emalie asked nervously.

"Oh, you know," Désirée purred, still smiling. "Some folks I know. Let's just say, I was the big winner. I've known you were special since the moment I first saw you." Désirée turned back to Oliver. "And no, Oliver, your little necklace wouldn't work on me, either. After all, I'm the one who sold it to Bane. Though he did do the hard work of getting it enchanted by Selene. Still, I would never sell something that could work against me. That would be like, oh, I don't know, having a friend who was the servant of your enemy."

Oliver grimaced. He felt the peculiar sensation that his head was an open book for Désirée to leaf through at her leisure.

"And where is your zombie friend?"

"He's busy," said Oliver simply.

"Oh, I see." Désirée grinned. "His Master's in town. And you don't like her. I can see why. So . . . I gather you met Selene. Couldn't save her, though." Désirée clucked her tongue against her teeth. "Pity."

"But," Oliver protested, "I didn't even know she was the Oracle that predicted my destiny. And I didn't know she needed saving. What was I supposed to do?"

"It's a good point," Désirée agreed. "Mess with Half-Light, and you might end up like your brother . . . though I assume that's why you're here. You want to save him?"

Oliver nodded. "We need to free him from a Nagual demon."

Désirée raised an eyebrow. "How daring. You'll have to go into the melded world of the jaguar and Bane to do it. The Nagual has bonded them, and lies within."

"You mean travel into Bane's head?" Oliver asked.

"The jaguar's and Bane's." Désirée turned to Emalie. "Much as you did before, when you were unraveling the mystery of your zombie friend's death."

"I can do that," said Emalie.

"Why of course you can. But I'm not sure you're ready for what you'll find in there."

"Like what?" Oliver asked.

Désirée winked. "Surprises." She spun and slipped into the shelves behind the counter. "For the Nagual, you'll need something specific."

Oliver turned and offered Emalie a shrug. But she was looking ahead, at the wall. He followed her gaze to that diamond-shaped mirror with the jade border. Oliver had seen Désirée gazing into it during past visits. From down here on the floor, they could only see the bright ceiling lights reflected in it. Except the lights seemed to be moving. It reminded Oliver of moonlight on water.

"Doesn't it look familiar to you?" Emalie whispered. "From —" .

"The museum." Oliver remembered now. The statue in Fortuna, of what had seemed to be Emalie's mom, only with the name Phoebe. That statue had been holding a diamond-shaped mirror. Phoebe's mirror had a handle, and it didn't have a jade border, as it was carved from white stone, but the angles of the diamond did look similar. And the round beveled edge of the border seemed similar, too.

"What's up with that?" Emalie asked.

Oliver wondered. He supposed he could just ask.

"I wouldn't." Désirée reappeared, her smile thinner, the faintest edge in her voice. "You can ask about anything you want on *that* side of the counter. What's on *this* side of the counter is my business."

"Sorry," Oliver mumbled.

"Why that's certainly all right, Oliver," Désirée replied, her voice instantly mild. "Now then . . ."

Her hands appeared from below the counter, and Oliver was surprised to see her place not a tiny bottle on the counter, but two swordlike weapons, each three feet long. They were made of wood, beginning with rounded handles. The main body was flattened and fat, with a square top. Along both edges, razor-sharp rectangles of obsidian glass protruded like teeth. The wood was painted with jaguar spots.

"These are Macuahuitl blades," said Désirée. "Lovely, aren't they?"

Oliver regarded them uncertainly. "We haven't had much experience with swords."

"You'd be surprised how quickly you learn when a Nagual is attacking you," Désirée responded. "But don't worry. These blades are imbued with the eternal jaguar spirit. When you are inside Bane and the jaguar's mind, you will find the jaguar's spirit guiding your hand. It should be fun."

"Great," mumbled Oliver.

"Now," Désirée continued, "the more important question would be how to carry these around." Désirée produced two small figurines: tiny jaguars made of a reddish basalt rock. The blades dissolved into smoke and seemed to be sucked into the statues.

"These will travel with you into Bane's head," she said, handing over the small statues. "When you need them, crush the figurines."

Oliver and Emalie each took one.

"That will be thirty-two myna," said Désirée pleasantly.

Oliver dug into his pocket and placed the square coins on the counter. When he looked up, Désirée was gone.

"She just vanished," Emalie murmured uncertainly.

"You'll need one more thing," Désirée called from somewhere behind them. Oliver and Emalie turned. "Over here."

They found her at the far end of an aisle, bent over and reaching into one of the shelves. As she pulled a small black bottle from the shelf and stood, Oliver saw a strange ruffling on the back of her lab coat, like a ridge of bumps on her spine, which made her coat catch.

"Your brother will be in quite a state when he is freed," said Désirée, handing Oliver the bottle. "Give him this tincture. It will help him recover. And it's free of charge."

"Thanks," said Oliver. He hesitated before leaving.

"Ahh, Oliver, always a lingering question in you, isn't there?" Oliver frowned. "Well," Désirée continued, "you're lucky I'm so patient. Ask away."

"Why did you want me to hear my prophecy? I mean, why did you want me to speak to Selene?"

"Well, just as I thought you deserved to know your origins, I also thought you had a right to know the true scope of your destiny," Désirée said kindly. "As I said before, you probably should have been told long before now. It's been such a shame, Oliver, how you've been kept in the dark."

Oliver almost laughed. Hadn't Désirée done her fair share of keeping him in the dark?

"Perhaps," she purred in answer to his thought, "but I have also championed your full awareness of your destiny and its meaning."

Oliver realized that she had a point. Who had really helped more than Désirée? Without her, where would he be? "But, like, if you can read my thoughts, then you know how all this is making me feel."

Désirée smiled. "Go on."

"Well —" Oliver figured there was no use lying to her. "It's all making me *not* want to fulfill the prophecy. Is that what you want?"

"Ahh," said Désirée. "See, that question is irrelevant, Oliver. I'm not concerned with what you want to do. I'm only concerned with what you *will* do."

"You make it sound like you already know," Oliver groaned wearily.

"I know a little," said Désirée coyly, "but mostly I am as intrigued as anyone. Now, go. You don't have much time to save your brother."

"Right." Oliver and Emalie started out.

"Until next time," said Désirée brightly.

CHAPTER 10

The Abandoned Lighthouse

"**I** can't believe we're gonna get to use swords," said Emalie as they rode atop a bus. The sky had cleared, a cold wind whisking the clouds away. There was no moon, and instead a rare view of the stars.

Oliver glanced at Emalie. She was squinting into the wind with a slight smile. "It's going to be dangerous," he replied cautiously.

"Come on," she said, punching his shoulder lightly. "We can handle it."

Something about this bothered Oliver. Should Emalie have been so *excited*? She'd always been daring — that was *one* word for bringing a camera into the Underground on her very first trip — but it seemed to be going further now. Trying to fool Désirée? Oliver felt a little lame for not being as enthusiastic as Emalie, but it just didn't feel right. A couple of hours ago she'd been totally down in the dumps, then giggling on the floor. It seemed

< 151 >

like the stronger she got, the more up-and-down she became as well.

"You're still worrying about Dean, aren't you?" Emalie asked.

"Even if the necklace works, we don't know for how long. And Lythia is strong."

"Well," said Emalie, "there he is. Let's go ask him." She pointed toward the sidewalk.

Sure enough, Dean was walking by with another figure.

Their bus passed him in a moment. Emalie winked out of sight. *Come on already!* She thought to him as she leaped off the bus.

Oliver jumped to his feet and followed.

Emalie popped back into sight on the sidewalk. "No problem," she said with a satisfied grin.

They hurried down the street, but then Oliver held out a hand to slow them down.

"Who's he with?" Emalie asked.

"Not sure. It's another zombie," said Oliver. "I can tell by the smell." At first, Oliver had thought it might be Autumn, but it wasn't.

"Well, let's go get him," said Emalie.

"Wait." Oliver held her back. "Let's see what they're up to for a minute first."

They stayed far back as Dean and his mystery companion walked. At one point the wind shifted. Oliver nodded to Emalie, then leaped up to a nearby roof, so that Dean wouldn't catch their scent. Emalie winked out of sight and joined him.

"It's almost like he's going to your house," Emalie commented after another mile.

"Yeah," said Oliver, but now he saw a more likely destination ahead. Sure enough, Dean crossed the street toward the bright neon island of 24-7 and Harvey's.

"Can we go in and see the blood racks?" Emalie asked as they approached the store.

"Some other time," Oliver replied, again noting her enthusiasm.

They kept out of line of the windows. Peering around a metal ice machine, they watched the front counter until Dean finally appeared carrying an armful of items. Tuna, baking soda, datura root . . .

"Those are the same things Lythia was buy —" Oliver began but stopped suddenly.

Dean's companion had joined him, and was gazing mildly out the window. Emalie's breath halted as well. He didn't see Oliver and Emalie, but they could see his face, and more important, the large wounds on his neck, now black and edged with mold after some time in the ground.

"That's the first jaguar victim," Oliver whispered gravely.

"I felt his spirit," said Emalie. "Dante, that was his name."

Dean paid for the items and the two walked toward the door, chatting with one another like regular friends.

Oliver tapped Emalie on the shoulder and they vaulted up to the roof.

"So, this means . . ." said Emalie.

"Yeah, it's Lythia," Oliver agreed. "She would've needed to be at the jaguar killing in order to prepare Dante for being raised. That's right, the baking soda she bought."

"What?"

"It's used to mask the presence of certain enchanted chemicals," said Oliver, putting the pieces together. "Bane attacks the victim, but then Lythia is the real killer. She uses her zombie serum, and tops it off with the baking soda to erase the presence. The vampire bite marks were probably her, too."

"You think she has Bane?"

Oliver nodded. "Her dad is the one who got the Nagual. She's probably been in charge of controlling the jaguar and where the killings happen, working for Half-Light."

"Then maybe Dean will lead us right to her."

"Yeah."

They leaped off the roof and followed Dean and Dante, heading west. After an hour, they wound up a quiet street lined with expensive homes. Beyond the last house, the street turned to dirt and entered thick trees wrapped in leafy vines. Soon they reached a rusted chain-link fence, and a gate. Dean and Dante vaulted over and headed inside.

Oliver and Emalie did the same. The road narrowed to rutted tire tracks, twisting through deep forest, rising gradually. High mounds of blackberry bushes loomed on either side of the road. The air was thick with the pungent aroma of ripe and decaying fruit.

Oliver couldn't help glancing into the growth, wary of jaguar eyes.

A rumble reached their ears and headlights flashed through the leaves. "Someone's coming," Oliver said. The blackberries were thick with thorns on either side. Oliver looked up and spied a wide branch high above the road. "There," he said. He shot up, grabbing the branch just as the vehicle rounded a bend. He could feel the prickle in his mind that meant Emalie was beside him.

The white news van passed below them. Oliver and Emalie had to pick up their feet to avoid the array of antennae on the top. They dropped back to the road and followed the receding red taillights.

Moments later, they emerged on a wide, clear plateau. Grass fields sloped down to a bluff, where flat concrete buildings were embedded in the earth. Beyond that was blackness, dotted with lights. A stiff breeze whipped their hair and carried the scent of salt water.

"Those look like bunkers," said Emalie, "like the World War II ones out on the islands. But I haven't been to these before."

To the right, a lighthouse stood on the crest of the field, its beacon off. The news truck had pulled up in front of it. Beyond it was a line of old barracks, their windows boarded up.

Oliver and Emalie stayed by the edge of the trees and approached through the tall grass. Oliver saw Karma and her cameraman standing outside the lighthouse.

"Let's start with a shot here before they arrive," said Karma. A light atop the camera illuminated her face as she spoke into her microphone. "A week of terror in Seattle came to an end tonight, when police and animal control tracked the escaped jaguar to this abandoned military station."

Oliver turned to Emalie and spectralized. *We have to get inside.*

Emalie winked out of sight. *Roger.*

Oliver slipped around behind Karma, giving her camera light a wide berth. They moved onto the porch of the lighthouse. The door was unlocked and squealed as

< 156 >

Oliver pushed it open. The inside was dark. Rooms to either side were vacant, trash and discarded pieces of lumber and furniture scattered across the warped floors.

They moved ahead and found what had once been a kitchen, its floor littered with smashed dishes. At the end of the hall, a spiral staircase led up into the light tower. Oliver peered up it but heard only the rustling of pigeons.

Over here, thought Emalie. Oliver turned and saw an open door at the far end of the kitchen. Faint light spilled from it.

They were almost to the door when Oliver heard more engines in the distance. He turned to a window, its glass gone, and looked through a wide crack in the boards. A black limousine had emerged from the woods.

Half-Light, Oliver thought worriedly.

They ducked through the doorway and down steep, rickety stairs to a concrete hallway. Naked bulbs hung from the ceiling, casting yellow light through grimy glass.

Voices echoed from ahead. Oliver heard the growl of the jaguar. He paused beside an open doorway, as one voice spoke loudly.

"Well now, kitty, guess who's arrived?" said Lythia. "What a treat we have for you!"

In here! Oliver thought and ducked through the doorway into a small, bare concrete room.

They hid in the dark as Lythia strode past, her boots cracking sharply on the floor. Oliver braced for their discovery. Spectralization wouldn't be enough to hide from a vampire with a demon, unless her mind was occupied by other things. Luckily that seemed to be the case, as she hurried up the stairs, and her footsteps echoed across the kitchen.

Oliver and Emalie continued down the hall to the only lit doorway and peered inside. The room was split in half by jail bars. On one side was the jaguar, pacing back and forth, eyes glowing orange. On the other were Dean and Dante, opening the cans of tuna.

"I think the Seahawks have a shot this year," Dante was saying casually.

"Maybe. They need a new running back," Dean replied. Zombies were big fans of American football, and wrestling, too, so this was a completely normal conversation for them to be having. But still, it bothered Oliver. It made Dean seem so different. *Like I don't know him at all,* Oliver thought darkly.

Hey, he's still Dean, Emalie thought at him sharply.

Yeah, well . . .

What do you want to do? Emalie asked.

Not sure yet. Oliver reached into his pocket for the necklace. *Maybe —*

"Hey, Dean." Emalie had stepped into the room and reappeared.

The zombies turned. Dean looked at her blankly.

"It's okay, we're here to get Bane out —"

Dean made a snarling sound, dropped the can opener and tuna, and lunged. He slammed into Emalie and they crashed to the floor.

"Dean, wait!" Oliver appeared in the room. The jaguar roared. Dante rushed at Oliver, who dodged out of the way and spun, grabbing the zombie and slamming him headfirst into the wall. Dante crumpled to the ground, leaving a dent in the concrete.

Dean had Emalie pinned, hands to her throat. She punched him in the shoulder, then the face, but Dean barely flinched. "Dean!" she gasped. Her face was beet red, her eyes wide with shock.

Oliver pulled out the necklace and dropped it around Dean's neck. There was a sizzling hiss. Dean shook his head. "Whu —" he saw Emalie, his hands on her neck, and threw himself backward, sliding across the floor.

Oliver bent to help Emalie, but she slapped his hand away and pushed herself to her feet, her face still red, hair wild, and her eyes thin and cold, glaring at Dean. "It's *me*," she said hoarsely.

Dean was looking around like his head was on a spring. "Emalie, sorry . . . Oliver. Where . . . jaguar? Oh . . ." He reached down and held the necklace, then tucked it in his shirt and looked up at Oliver guiltily. "Thanks."

Oliver nodded grimly. He wanted badly to forget the image of Dean choking Emalie but felt like he might not for a long time. "I don't know how long the necklace will work for," he said, avoiding Dean's eyes. "So, how do we get out of here?"

"Right," Dean said, gathering himself. "Okay, I think the passages will get us out, but . . . it's foggy, whenever I'm working . . ."

"Working?" Emalie asked.

"Sorry, I mean, you know, when my master has me doing stuff."

"Can't you just call her Lythia?" Emalie said sourly.

"I prefer 'Master.'"

Oliver and Emalie spun to find Lythia in the doorway.

"Yes, Master," Dean mumbled.

Oliver glared back at him.

"Sorry!" Dean pleaded. "It's habit!"

"Tsk tsk, Oliver," Lythia said. "Why would you come here? Didn't I tell you that I was going to save you?"

Oliver tried desperately to find a response.

"Yeah, right," Emalie spat.

"Quiet, blood bag," Lythia snapped. "Poor Oliver. You probably think you're doing the right thing, trying to save big brother. But you don't know what he was really up to."

"I don't care," Oliver shot back. "I'm not going to believe anything you say."

Lythia smiled. Her teeth were freshly coated in magenta glitter that matched her hair. "Have it your way, but it doesn't matter. Tyrus and my father are here, and they'll be dealing with Bane quite permanently."

"Why are you doing this?" Oliver asked.

"Not telling," Lythia said. "Minion!"

"Yes, Master. . . ." Dean mumbled.

"Dean —" Oliver began.

"It's no use, Oliver," Lythia purred. "He's my toy, not yours. Take the blood bag here and throw her in the cell."

Dean grabbed Emalie.

"Dean, stop!" Emalie shouted.

Lythia stepped toward the cage. "Let's give the poor kitty boy one last snack."

Oliver watched in horror. The necklace must not have been strong enough. He lunged at Lythia, slamming into her. They stumbled across the room and ended up face-to-face against the wall.

"See, Oliver?" Lythia murmured, her eyes blazing in lavender glow. "I knew you liked me."

"Shut UP!" Oliver yelled, but felt a second of that usual foggy-headedness that Lythia and her demon caused.

That was all Lythia needed. She hurled him across the room and he crashed into the wall, his shoulder exploding in pain as he crumpled to the floor atop the unconscious zombie.

Lythia brushed herself off and typed on a small keypad on the cell. The locks clicked open. The jaguar turned and crouched, hissing, ears back. "All right, kitty," said Lythia. "Time for a big treat." She glanced back at Dean, who had Emalie by the arms. "Excellent." She pushed open the cell door and turned to grab Emalie. "Well done, Min —"

Dean's fist hurtled through the air. It caught Lythia in the temple, and her whole body was thrown, rocketing backward into the cell, where she slumped over, eyes closed.

"I'm not your minion," Dean muttered, letting go of Emalie as he did so.

Oliver staggered to his feet. Dean reached out a hand to right him. "Nice," Oliver mumbled, rubbing his shoulder.

"That felt good," Dean agreed.

Oliver turned to the cage. "Bane," he called.

The jaguar growled menacingly.

"Bane, I know you hear me. We have to get you out of here —"

The jaguar lunged, knocking Oliver to the floor and roaring in his face.

"Bane! You have to get control!" Oliver shouted desperately.

"He can't," said Dean. He ducked into the cage and rooted through Lythia's pockets. "The Nagual is too strong. Here." He stood, holding a small statue. It had a tiny feline body and an oversized, demonic head, with an angry face of wild eyes and gritted teeth. "It's the totem that controls the Nagual. Obey!" he shouted.

The jaguar whipped its head around, hissing at Dean, but backed off of Oliver.

Dean moved to the door. "Come on, kitty." He started down the hall. The jaguar slunk out of the room after him.

Oliver turned to Emalie. "Ready —" he began, only to find Emalie reaching into her bag and producing her stake, whittled from a hammer handle. She started toward Lythia, her eyes cold.

CHAPTER 11

The Lair of the Nagual

"**W**ait!" Oliver grabbed Emalie's arm.

She shot an icy glare at him. "What?" She tried to shake her arm free, but Oliver held her firmly.

"You can't," he said, frowning. "It will destroy Dean."

Emalie lowered the stake reluctantly. "But I *really* don't like her."

"Neither do I. Come on."

Emalie sighed but let Oliver pull her back out. As they left the cell, she slammed the door shut. Lythia didn't stir.

They ran down the hall, following the scent of Dean and the jaguar. The string of lightbulbs ended, and they ran on through darkness. The air grew wet and cool.

"This way," a voice called from beside them.

Oliver and Emalie halted, finding Dean and the jaguar in a small side passage. "I remember going this way," said Dean, leading on. "When I was doing something for Lythia. I think it's a way out."

Oliver glanced over his shoulder. "We're not going to have long before Lythia comes to, or Tyrus comes after us. We've got to free Bane."

Dean hurried ahead, the jaguar trotting at his heels. "This will work."

Moments later they reached the tunnel's end. A metal ladder led up to a wooden trapdoor.

"Head up there and get things ready. Then I'll call him up."

Oliver and Emalie climbed, pushed open the trapdoor, and emerged in a dark, cobwebbed basement with a dirt floor. Faint evening light shone through small, grimy windows.

Emalie pulled a glass bottle from her bag and began pouring a circle of gypsum sand on the ground, right beside the trapdoor. She moved away from it and sat. "That's for the jaguar," she said. She traded the sand bag for a weathered gray coin: the memory rite that she'd used to enter Oliver's head back in the winter. "Put that in the circle," she said.

"What memory are we going into?" Oliver asked, confused.

"I don't know," said Emalie. "One of Bane's . . . whichever one we're drawn to. The memory rite is the only way I know to bring you guys into his head with me. Désirée made it sound like we were all supposed to go in."

"Yeah," Oliver agreed. "But Bane's inside an animal. Do you think it will even work?"

"You're always worrying," Emalie said with a smile, but also with less of her bravado than before.

Oliver placed the rite in the sand circle, then turned to see Emalie dabbing small drops of liquid from a silver flask onto her wrists. She put out a hand. Oliver took it. Their other two hands were outstretched for Dean.

"Okay!" Emalie called.

Dean leaped up out of the trapdoor and sat down beside them, grabbing their hands. "Sasha, come!" he called.

The jaguar lunged up out of the hole, landing in the circle. It looked around, and hissed.

Then there was a rush of darkness.

❀

Oliver wasn't sure what he'd been expecting, maybe something like the trip into *his* memory, where they'd ended up in a version of his school.

Instead, they found themselves gazing out at the night skyline of Seattle, its lights sparkling and refracted by raindrops. Clouds rushed across the building tops. Rain pelted their faces.

Oliver had a moment of panic — they seemed to be in midair — but then looked down to find his feet planted on a carpeted floor. Teeth of broken glass angled up just beyond his toes — a floor-to-ceiling window that had been smashed. The side of a building fell away beyond that. Strangely, the street far below glittered with police lights.

Sirens wailed in the distance.

"Where are we?" Dean asked.

Emalie and Dean were on either side of Oliver, looking around and trying to figure out their surroundings. More than just this window had been destroyed. The entire wall in either direction had been blown apart. Only twisted metal beams and glass shards remained. Oliver had already counted the rows of windows across the street and guessed that they were on the twenty-third floor.

"Whoa," Emalie gasped. She'd turned around.

Oliver did the same. They were standing in what might have once been an office, only most of the walls were gone, the furniture charred, splintered, melted. Everything was dark except for the occasional electric spark from a stray wire. Tiny pockets of flame flickered here and there.

"This must have been some party," Dean commented dryly.

Emalie started into the devastation. Oliver and Dean followed.

They picked their way down a long, destroyed hallway

littered with debris. With each step away from the out-side walls of the building, the air grew warmer and more humid. Emalie reached out to the blackened wall and touched a long vine of thick green leaves.

"What's with that?" Dean asked.

"This is what Désirée meant," said Emalie. "We're in Bane's mind, but we're in the jaguar's, too." As they walked, the leafy vines increased, winding through the blasted walls, twisting across the floor. Oliver heard a sound like crickets, and a bird call.

The hallway ended and the three stopped. Before them was an enormous chamber. It seemed as if the building had been hollowed out for five floors, up to the triangular roof, where large skylights had smashed and now allowed a light rain to fall inside. Three levels of balconies ringed the space, ornately decorated like those in a fancy theater, but large sections had collapsed or hung cockeyed from the explosion. All the windows were blown out. There was an enormous fountain on the floor, buried in rubble.

Atop all of this were coils of slithering vines. Thick trees snaked up the walls. Birds called from the rafters. A small waterfall cascaded down one of the collapsed balconies, creating a tropical pool lined with flowers among the concrete debris.

"Where are we?" Dean asked.

"I don't know," said Oliver. But the place did seem somehow familiar to him.

"Charles!" Oliver whirled to see Phlox standing up from the wreckage, throwing aside a large piece of concrete. She was dressed in a formal black gown, her hair up, but covered in dust.

"She's part of Bane's memory," Emalie whispered.

"Phlox." Sebastian appeared, clambering over the wreckage on one of the balconies. He had Tyrus over his shoulder. Both their tuxedoes were singed and torn. Sebastian leaped down to the floor, laying Tyrus on a collapsed table. "Where is he?"

"I don't know . . ." Phlox stumbled about, digging through the rubble. "Charles!"

"I remember this," Oliver whispered, even though the people in Bane's memory wouldn't have heard him. "I remember my parents coming home from this night. It was awhile ago . . . something like fifteen human years, give or take . . . and yeah, I know this building. Of course, the twenty-third floor. My parents and Bane came. It was before he got his demon."

"So you're not in this memory?" Emalie asked.

"No, I was still too young to attend the ball."

"The ball?"

"The Darkling Ball," Oliver explained, "for the Festival of Waning Sun."

"Isn't that the thing that's coming up next month, for you?" said Dean. "Where you're going to get all powered up by that demon lady?"

"Vyette," said Oliver. "Yeah."

"Here he is!" Sebastian shouted in the memory. Oliver saw him digging into the rubble and pulling Bane free. Bane was also dressed formally, but unconscious and badly wounded. He looked so young.

"That's right," said Oliver, remembering. "Bane was at the doctor for, like, weeks after that. He got hurt bad."

"What happened to this place?"

"There was an explosion," said Oliver. "I don't think my parents told me exactly what happened —"

"I found Ravonovich!" They looked up to see Leah calling down from one of the balconies. "He —" But Leah couldn't finish. Suddenly, thick vines wrapped around her and sucked her down into the rubble.

"Um . . ." Dean began.

There was a great slithering sound, and Sebastian and Phlox were wrapped in vines as well. They didn't protest, but rather froze in place as they were pulled down into the wreckage because, Oliver guessed, the vines weren't part of Bane's memory. Tyrus was dragged out of sight as well.

Bane remained lying there, out cold.

"He changed," said Emalie.

Oliver saw that Bane had morphed into his current self. The tuxedo had been replaced by his black jeans and a tight T-shirt. Green stripes appeared in his hair.

"What just happened?" asked Dean.

A terrible, shredding hiss tore through the silence. "I think that did," said Emalie. Oliver and Dean followed her gaze into the dark shadows on the far end of the chamber. Two fiery orange eyes lit in the darkness. There was a scraping sound, like claws on stone, and suddenly a smoky black form lunged, landing in front of them.

"So, that's probably the Nagual," guessed Oliver.

The creature was ten feet tall, standing upright on thick hind legs. Its face was feline as well, but also covered in spikes like a *vampyr* demon. Its body was a cross between a giant cat and a human, yet its features were hard to make out. It seemed to be composed of smoke, except for its huge claws and jaws, which looked very solid and lethal. It unleashed a grating, deafening cry.

"Time for these," said Oliver, and pulled out his jaguar statue. Emalie did the same.

"What are those?" asked Dean.

"Now," said Oliver, and the two hurled the statues against the ground. They exploded into jets of fog, which slipped up to their hands and formed the obsidian-studded Aztec blades.

"Hey!" Dean whined, eyes wide. "Why don't *I* get a sword?"

"Sorry," said Oliver.

Seeing these, the Nagual howled viciously.

"You might be glad you don't have one," said Emalie nervously.

The Nagual hurled itself forward.

The three scattered. Oliver dove, slashing with his blade as he did. The sword sunk deep into the smoky torso of the creature — but slipped right through. The Nagual's body rippled in its wake and re-formed.

"I don't think the swords work!" Oliver shouted, and then was slammed in the back by the creature's enormous paw. Its claws tore at his skin.

"That's not fair!" Dean shouted. "How come it can hit back?" He vaulted onto one of the balconies, grabbed a table-sized chunk of staircase, and hurled it down at the creature. It struck the Nagual in the chest, but passed right through, the creature instantly re-forming.

It turned toward Emalie and swiped. She blinked out of sight and reappeared a few feet away, swinging her sword and connecting with the Nagual's paw just as it passed. There was a crunch of blade against claw, and the Nagual reared back and screamed in rage.

"That works!" she shouted, but was immediately slammed by another blow and thrown into the air, plunging into the tropical pool.

"Dean!" Oliver shouted. "Keep it occupied!"

"Great!" Dean replied. "No problem!"

Oliver scrambled across the ruins, angling toward Emalie, who was dragging herself up from the water.

The Nagual had turned toward her, fangs bared, and Oliver leaped high, swinging his sword at its head. The obsidian blades connected with its skull in a vicious clang. The creature roared in rage.

Oliver landed and turned to see it spinning toward him, but Dean hurled a heavy, metal theater seat and connected with its head. "Here, kitty!" Dean shouted. The creature staggered, spun, and flew up onto the balcony in a jet of smoke. "Uh . . ." Dean turned and leaped up to a higher one.

Oliver reached Emalie as she was getting to her feet, her clothes dripping.

"You okay?"

"Fine. You?" she asked heavily, pushing soaked hair from her eyes.

"Yeah." Oliver looked over at Bane. "Is that really him?"

"Yeah, I think this memory is where the Nagual has been keeping him captive," said Emalie. "We need to get him out of here."

"Back to the spot where we entered?"

"I think so." Emalie started climbing toward Bane.

"Whoa!" They looked up to see Dean tumbling

through the air along with the crumbling remains of a high balcony, the Nagual diving after him. He landed hard on the balcony below, but jumped to his feet. "Can we *go* now?" he shouted at Emalie and Oliver.

They reached Bane and knelt beside him. "Bane," said Oliver. "Wake up."

Bane stirred, wincing.

"We have to get you out of here."

One eye squinted open, and Bane regarded Oliver. "What are you doing in here?" he said groggily.

"We're here to rescue you from the Nagual." Oliver started pulling Bane up by the arm.

"Just leave me here, bro," Bane groaned. "What's the point. . . . This is where it all ended, anyway. . . ."

Oliver didn't know what he was talking about. "No, Bane, we're getting you out. You've been tricked by Half-Light, set up, and they're coming for you." He pulled Bane to his feet.

They scrambled back across the wreckage, toward the hallway they'd entered from. Dean dropped to the floor beside them. "Going? Great!"

There was an earsplitting hiss, and the Nagual landed right in front of them, blocking their way, claws and fangs bared.

"Here." Oliver pushed Bane against Dean and lashed forward with his sword. The Nagual caught him in the side and leveled him. The sword clattered free.

"Now what?" Dean shouted. The Nagual blasted them with another spitting roar, and swiped at Emalie and Dean. They fell down in a heap, along with Bane. The Nagual pounced onto them, claws tearing.

"No!" Oliver jumped up, grabbing his sword and spinning to attack — when a brilliant red light blazed forth from beneath the Nagual. Oliver staggered back, throwing a hand over his eyes, practically blinded.

The creature lurched away, its eyes also blinking uselessly. Emalie stood up before it, and Oliver saw that she was holding Bane's limp hand. Her eyes had turned bloodred again, the pupils white. Red light radiated from her entire body, blazing so hot it was turning white.

"Get away, demon!" she ordered, her voice edged with piercing, high-pitched overtones. It sounded like three of her speaking at once, the others something more than human.

The Nagual looked confused, but then lashed out at her. Emalie swung her sword with her other hand, and it burned with white-hot light, digging into the Nagual's torso.

There was an explosion of light, fire, and swirling smoke, and Oliver's vision was completely overwhelmed. The Nagual screamed hideously.

"Leave this creature and this vampire!" Emalie's voice sounded barely like her own.

A swirling wind kicked up in the room. The Nagual's wail grew deafening.

Oliver fell to his knees, his eyes useless. The wind burned his face.

Then it died out. The light darkened.

Oliver, he heard in his mind, and looked up. His vision was washed in green, dark at its edges, yet there was something still glowing brightly in front of him . . . human in form. It reminded Oliver of the apparition. *It's me* . . . Oliver thought he recognized the voice. From where? Then the light faded further and he saw the outline of Emalie within it. She was holding out her hand to him. Oliver felt confused. From the sound of the voice, he had expected someone else, but he couldn't quite place who.

He took Emalie's hand and got to his feet.

"I'm fine, really," said Dean, stumbling over, blinking madly and holding Bane on his shoulder.

Oliver peered at Emalie. She looked like herself again, with a few loose strands of hair pulled from her braids. Her pupils had returned to black, yet her irises were still bloodred. "What did you do?" he asked.

Emalie glanced at Bane. "I channeled his demon, I think. I knew it from before . . . from the museum in Italy, and from the other night at the playground. So I just called to it, and told it to help me."

"You *told* Bane's *vampyr* to help you?" Oliver asked incredulously. "And it listened to you? And you're alive?"

Emalie half smiled. "Seems like it. I don't really remember what I did after that, except that we both wanted that Nagual out of here . . . so we focused on that."

"Okay," said Oliver dumbly. She'd referred to herself and Bane's *vampyr* as "we." Oliver had never heard of any such thing.

"Hey, let's figure all this out once we're out of here, huh?" said Dean.

"Right." Oliver dropped his sword, took one of Bane's arms, and they started back to the hallway.

"Leave me here," Bane mumbled weakly, barely keeping his feet beneath him.

"No," Oliver replied curtly.

Emalie led the way down the hall. Oliver watched her, still baffled by what she'd just done.

And then he saw something he understood even less. "Hold on."

A glimpse of a familiar shape had caught his eye. Oliver reached toward the blasted-out, vine-covered wall. He peeled away the leafy growth. There stood a warped, faded wooden door. There was a Skrit carved into it, with only remnants of the original white paint still visible in its lines:

Oliver felt a rush inside, like a yawning wind. He'd seen this before. He took the tarnished silver door handle and entered the room.

"Yeah, I'm going to wait here," said Dean. "I've had enough of your brother's mind."

Oliver heard Emalie's footsteps follow.

They entered a small, spare room. There was a desk covered in dust. An overturned office chair. The floor was strewn with books, all fallen off the shelves. On the back wall was a large, diamond-shaped window. Through its clouded glass, Oliver saw red lands and a starry, crystal black sky. There was a pyramid of gleaming jade in the distance. Lying nearby was the head of a huge, amethyst statue. It had gold eyes that gleamed like coins.

"Those stars," said Emalie quietly. "Those are the constellations I made above my bed. Where is this place?"

"It's Nexia," said Oliver. "There's a room like this in

my head." He stepped closer to the window. Except for the condition, everything about this room was the same. Only one thing was missing. He peered out the window in either direction. The Gate was nowhere to be found.

This is my place in your mind, Illisius, Oliver's soon-to-be demon, had told him back in the winter. Was this where Bane's *vampyr* demon lived? But why a view of Nexia? Why the same symbol on the door?

"I don't get it," Emalie began. "Oh . . ."

Oliver tore his gaze away from the plains of Nexia — it wasn't easy — to see Emalie looking down at her shirt. A bright streak of crimson had dripped onto her vest. When she looked up again, he saw a long gash across her chin.

"What happened?" he asked.

Emalie's eyes widened. "Outside . . . back with our bodies . . . something's there!"

"Ow!" Dean shouted from out in the hall. "Why does my head hurt?"

"We have to get out!" Emalie ran back into the hall.

Oliver longed to stay, to understand, but — his shoulder exploded in pain again, as if he'd been struck. He raced down the hall, joining Emalie, Dean, and Bane at the edge of the blasted-out window. They joined hands, Oliver getting one last glimpse of the melee of police activity far below, and then everything dissolved in a swirl.

Oliver looked up to see the ceiling of the barracks house. He sat up, hearing a strange scraping sound like dirt moving — only to be slammed back to the ground.

The jaguar was lying motionless in the sand circle. Oliver spied Bane lying nearby, shivering. There was Emalie, sitting up. And there was Dean, flying across the room and slamming into the wall as if he'd been thrown. As he fell to the floor, he found Oliver. "Sorry!" he shouted.

"What?" Oliver asked, scrambling to his feet.

"Well," said Dean. "I think I remember why Lythia had me coming to this place."

Oliver turned and saw the source of the strange sound. The earth was moving. Now a rotten hand burst from the soil. Then another, clawing out. A head of dirt-matted black hair appeared, and then the face of the third jaguar victim, now a zombie, her eyes, nose, and mouth still full of soil.

"I think I buried these guys here," said Dean. "My bad."

Oliver heard thudding footsteps and looked up to see the second zombie victim racing toward them.

Chapter 12

The Forgotten Graveyard

"**E**malie!" Oliver shouted.

"What?" said Emalie wearily, wiping at her bloody chin.

Oliver dove, gliding over Emalie. He caught the large, overweight zombie boy in the chest and tackled him to the floor. Oliver immediately jumped up and ran for Bane.

"Where are your swords?" Dean shouted.

"They only work in the jaguar!" Oliver replied, sliding to his knees beside Bane.

"Oh, great," Dean muttered.

Oliver bent over his brother. "Come on! Bane, get up."

Bane looked around weakly, but managed to get his feet beneath him.

"Dah!" Emalie shouted as the zombie girl grabbed at her. She jumped away and winked out of sight.

Oliver dragged Bane toward the rickety staircase. Dirty fingernails raked down his back. He turned to find the two zombies lurching toward him.

Dean jumped between them. "Hey, guys," he said reasonably. "Let's not do this, okay? I know you guys are just raised and probably really hungry — I get that — but they're with me."

The zombie girl grabbed Dean by the hair and tore a chunk out.

"Ow!" He shoved her across the room and spun around. "Okay, fine! Time to go!"

They scrambled up the stairs, Oliver helping Bane, then hurried down the hall toward the front door of the barracks. Oliver sped up to slam through the door.

Suddenly the floor exploded, and the female zombie burst up into the room. She looked at Oliver, then sniffed at the air. "Brains . . ." she said hungrily.

"Oh come on," Dean moaned. "You're giving us all a bad name."

The zombie girl lunged to Oliver's side.

Guh!

Emalie popped back into view as the zombie fell on top of her. Like Dean, these zombies could see through enchantments.

Oliver reached for her, only to be sent staggering by a vicious blow from the zombie boy, lumbering down the hall behind them.

"Minions! Heel!"

Oliver looked up to see the front door of the barracks open. Tyrus and Lythia stood there.

"Back away," Lythia ordered, and the two zombies retreated toward the wall, the girl snarling, the boy panting.

Tyrus stepped inside, avoiding the zombie-made hole in the floor. He surveyed Oliver and his friends with a frown. "Bane, I'll need you to come with me."

Bane looked up through his wild hair. "Where?" he said weakly.

"Somewhere safe," said Tyrus. "Somewhere you can recover." Tyrus glanced at Oliver, then back to Bane. "We know what you were planning for Oliver. We know all of it. You need help."

Bane glared at Tyrus. "Help," he muttered. "Sure."

"Your parents agree with me."

"No they don't!" Oliver shouted. "Bane, don't listen to him."

"Yes, Bane, they do," said Tyrus. "Oliver, I know this all seems strange to you, but it's for the best."

"You lied to my parents," Oliver shot back.

"I didn't have a choice," said Tyrus defensively. "We all answer to Half-Light. Your parents know that. They knew the game."

"This isn't a game!" Oliver shouted. "I'm not a game! Bane's not a game!"

"Forget it, bro," said Bane. "They can take me."

"No, they can't."

"Oliver, I'm afraid I have t —" Suddenly Tyrus buckled sideways and crumpled to the floor.

Behind him, Lythia lowered a heavy length of board. Oliver gaped at her incredulously.

Lythia only smiled. "I told you I was here to save you, Oliver. I've been waiting for the right moment to slip from Half-Light's sight. They are sooo overbearing. Anyway, except for a few bumps in the road, this has turned out just like I hoped."

"Like we'd believe you," said Emalie.

Lythia rolled her eyes. "Oh, blood bag . . ." she said and turned back to Oliver. "Come with me and I'll save you, just like I said."

Oliver shook his head. "There's no way."

Lythia's eyes narrowed. "How about if I force you to? Minions."

Lythia and the two zombies stepped toward them. Oliver readied himself for another fight, when he heard a low, vibrating growl. Lythia paused and glanced down at the hole in the floor.

"Sasha," Dean said softly. Oliver glanced over to see Dean holding the totem. "Attack."

Lythia had just enough time to look up and start to smile. "I'm impressed."

The jaguar lunged up from the darkness, sinking its claws and teeth into Lythia's legs and dragging her down into the basement.

There was a snarling commotion from below.

"Minions! A little help!" Lythia shouted.

The two zombies immediately jumped down the hole. Dean twitched like he was about to follow, but gritted his teeth and managed to stay where he was, looking relieved.

"Can we watch?" Emalie asked, peering after them.

"No, we need to get Bane out of —" Oliver looked around. Bane was gone. "Where'd he go?"

There was a crack of splintering wood from the back of the barracks. Oliver, Emalie, and Dean rushed down the hall to find a door by the kitchen tossed aside. Stepping out onto the back porch, they spotted Bane sprinting away across the dark field, toward the bluff.

They raced after him across the wet grass. Ahead, Oliver saw Bane disappear over the bluff edge. They reached it in moments and halted. A long, steep hill of clay and bushes fell to a narrow strip of gray beach. Tiny waves lapped at its pebbled shores. Bane was nowhere to be seen.

"Maybe he needs some alone time?" suggested Dean.

"Bane," Oliver muttered. "We can't let Half-Light find him first."

"Can't find his scent," said Dean. The wind was whipping in off the sound, where banks of fog rolled along the water.

Oliver turned to Emalie. "Can you sense him?"

"I don't think so," said Emalie. Oliver noticed that she was shivering badly.

"Are you okay?"

She looked at him seriously. "I'm not sure. I feel a little weird."

"I know where he's going." Jenette's smoky form suddenly appeared between them. "Sorry I didn't get here sooner," she said, a slight pout to her voice. "I wish you guys would call me for your big adventures."

"Hi," said Oliver. He wondered how Jenette even knew where to find them, or what they'd been up to. "How do you know where Bane is?"

"Follow me," Jenette said simply, and slithered down the bluff.

Oliver turned to Emalie and Dean and shrugged, then jumped off the bluff edge, sailing down to the beach. Emalie appeared beside him. Dean tumbled down, covered in sand.

"This way," said Jenette, floating up the beach.

As they walked, the fog began to roll in, breaths of cool droplets obscuring their view.

"How do you know where Bane's going?" Oliver asked again.

"Well . . . I've been there with him before," Jenette replied. "Don't you remember?"

"What are you talking about?"

"Oh, that's right, I keep forgetting," said Jenette.

"Keep forgetting what?"

"Well . . . there's this thing. I want to tell you, but I can't. Not yet."

Oliver threw up his hands. "Great. Join the club."

"You could charge, like, dues," Dean piped up sarcastically. "People should have to pay for the right to keep you in the dark all the time. You'd be rich."

Emalie snickered just loud enough for Jenette to hear. Oliver noticed she was still shivering.

"Come on, you guys," Jenette groaned. "It's not like that, I swear."

"Everybody could get charged interest, you know, like on how long they lie to you," Dean went on. "We could have my dad run the club. He's an accountant."

"Yeah," Oliver said, feeling a hint of relaxation creep through his sore body. Then his foot crunched on something, and he stopped in his tracks.

"This is the place," Jenette whispered from beside him.

Oliver found himself standing in a pile of splintered wood, fabric, and bones.

Looking ahead, Oliver spied another similar pile. Smashed coffins, lying on the beach. Waves lapped against the boards. Crabs scuttled among the bones and tattered clothing. There was a larger collapsed structure of cement and columns: a mausoleum.

"Whoa," said Dean.

Oliver followed his gaze upward. High on the steep bluff, wrapped in fog, Oliver saw objects protruding from the earth at odd angles. Coffins, the earth having eroded away around them. Some looked ready to fall.

"Up here," said Jenette, and began rising up the slope.

Oliver reached out for the forces and levitated. Dean scrambled up the clay, grabbing on to tangles of brush. Emalie blinked away and reappeared beside Oliver as he reached the top.

They stood at the edge of an overgrown field. A few large, old trees spread a wide canopy of branches over tangles of shrubs and blackberry vines. Moldy, moss-covered tombstones were barely visible within the vegetation.

"This cemetery's probably not on our map," commented Dean.

"That's the point," said Jenette. "This way." She floated forward, along a narrow dirt path through the growth.

They weaved through the dark, silent graveyard. An owl called. The high-pitched whispers of bats echoed above. The silence seemed intentional, like the dead were watching them walk by, and listening. They couldn't help stepping lightly.

Now Oliver heard a sound ahead. Mumbling . . .

They reached the edge of a clearing. The treetops were still thick overhead, but here, the vines and bushes gave way to a circle of grass.

In the center was a depression in the earth, before a tombstone. A figure was kneeling in the dirt, hunched over, muttering.

"Bane?" Oliver whispered. He started forward.

"Dude, what's he doing —" Dean began, but Emalie held him back.

"Let him go," Oliver heard Emalie say.

Oliver crossed the clearing alone, approaching Bane, and now he could make out some of his brother's words. "Now what do I have? What do I have?" He slammed his fist down against the soil.

Oliver stopped at the edge of the depression. It looked as if it had been dug by hand. He was about to say something when he saw the bones sticking out of the dirt. There were two sets of ribs, a pile of papers, and other debris cluttered within them. Above that were two skulls, staring up into the night with empty eyes. Oliver looked at the tombstone:

VICTOR WEISSEL, LOVING FATHER
1895 — 1921
IRENE WEISSEL, BELOVED MOTHER
1899 — 1921

And below that:

ELIJAH WEISSEL, CHILD OF GOD
1920-1921

"Bane . . ." Oliver said weakly, and in a cold rush, he
• understood a truth that had been right in front of him,
all along.

He stepped down into the depression, kneeling beside
his brother. He put a hand lightly on Bane's shoulder,
something he'd never done before, and braced for Bane
to knock it free, but he didn't. "They did it to you,
first," Oliver said carefully. Bane hadn't been jealous
that Oliver was the child chosen for the prophecy. "You
were the prophecy child."

Bane nodded.

"These were your human parents."

"I never even knew them," said Bane heavily.

"You . . ." Oliver struggled to turn his shock into
words. ". . . were sired just like me. And . . ."

"And I failed, bro," Bane finished. "The night of the
Darkling Ball, I was supposed to be anointed with

power, to travel to Nexia and meet Illisius. . . . But the room blew up . . . I was hurt too badly. . . . And that was it. Half-Light decided I was too weak to receive Illisius, that they were better off starting over." Bane's shoulders heaved. "I wasn't strong enough."

"But I'd already been sired," said Oliver.

Bane chuckled. "Yeah, you were the backup plan. Once I failed, they put another demon in me — just some average *vampyr* — and then I was no longer demonless, and so the prophecy passed to you."

Oliver couldn't believe it. All this time, all these years, Oliver had thought that he and Bane couldn't have been more different, and yet they were merely on opposite sides of the same cruel fate. Oliver remembered thinking that Bane would have been better suited to the prophecy than he was: And it was true. Bane *had* been, and now he'd been left bitterly behind as the prophecy moved on without him. Left behind to feel like he'd failed, like he hadn't been strong enough. And he had to watch as what had once been his was given to his younger brother.

Bane coughed wickedly. Oliver reached into his pocket and produced the small black bottle he'd gotten from Désirée.

"Here. This is supposed to help you recover from the jaguar."

< 191 >

Bane took the bottle, popped off the cork, and slugged it back. "Half-Light trapped me in there with that Nagual," he said.

"Yeah, they were framing you."

"Perfect." Bane dropped the bottle and wiped at his mouth. "That tasted terrible."

Oliver watched the bottle fall among the debris lying within the rib cages of Bane's parents, but he now saw that it wasn't trash at all. It was a collection of papers and clippings. Oliver noticed one faded yellow headline that read:

Explosion Rocks Historic Downtown Building

And then he spied another newspaper clipping that he'd seen before:

CHRISTMAS TRAGEDY:
Mother and Father Slain, Child Missing

Oliver could barely speak. He picked up the clipping. Oliver had thought it was Emalie who had placed a copy of this beneath his desk at school. But then Emalie had told him that someone had stolen it from her. He looked at Bane. "*You* gave me this."

Bane chuckled weakly. "What did I say, bro, that

night way back at the school? I said, *Big brother is here to help. . . .*" He coughed again.

"I thought," said Oliver, "I thought you were jealous. I thought you were trying to steal the prophecy, or make it your own, or something."

Bane laughed again. "That's hilarious." He turned to Oliver, and his gaze hardened. "I don't want the prophecy back."

"But then . . . why? Why have you been sneaking around learning about the prophecy? Why did you steal Selene's summoning charm? Why is Half-Light trying to frame you?"

"Because," said Bane, "I'm trying to free you from it."

"What?" Oliver couldn't believe it.

Bane almost grinned. "I know, right?"

"You —" Oliver felt something like anger. "But you're such a jerk to me."

"Well, that part's just for fun —"

"But that's what I want!" Oliver shouted. "I *want* to be free of the prophecy!"

Bane looked at him gravely. "I know you do."

Oliver threw up his hands. "Why would *you* want that?"

"Yeah, well," said Bane. "I guess because . . . you're my younger brother. I watch you. I see how hard it is for you, and I . . . I don't want you to end up like this . . . like me."

"But what's wrong with *you*? You're a normal vampire. I'm the one who's a screwup."

"Tsss." Bane's face soured. "I've never been right inside, bro. I always feel different, separated. . . . Like there's a glass wall between me and everybody else. You'd think it would have changed when I got my demon, and it did, kind of. With a demon, I don't feel as lonely anymore, but I'm still bitter, left out. Everyone else I know is out there being normal and I'm right there with them, acting the same way, but inside . . . it just doesn't work."

"But you always make fun of me for acting weird."

"Yeah, I thought it might help you straighten out. Guess not, huh?" Bane's face tightened. "The worst part is, I don't know when it's ever gonna end for me. Am I gonna be screwed up like this forever?" He turned to Oliver. "Are you?"

Oliver shivered at the thought.

"I don't want that for you, bro."

"But what about, like, freedom for the vampires and all that?"

"Bah," Bane grunted. "You heard what Grandma and the family said down in the Old World. What's so bad about this place? Blood and chaos whenever you want it. The fact that we might take a stake is what makes it fun, right? That's the whole point of Finity."

"Of what?" Oliver hadn't heard of Finity.

Bane chuckled weakly. "We'll talk. And besides, Half-Light doesn't even know if their big plan is going to work. They might be wrong about the prophecy, and where does that leave us? Face it. We're lab rats, bro, that's all we've ever been. Living in our little maze. It's too late for me, but not for you."

Oliver nodded, yet couldn't help asking, "Are you lying to me?"

"Ha. Good one. No. And if you tell anyone I said this stuff, I'll tear your tongue out."

"Okay . . ." Oliver said, stunned by it all. "So, there's really a way? To undo the prophecy?"

"Yeah," said Bane. "Selene told me. And I've been working on it. Things were almost ready, then I was gonna tell you, but I got careless. Lythia jumped me at the zoo and I lost my necklace. Half-Light probably already suspected what I was up to, but then they were sure. And next thing I knew, I was in the jaguar with the Nagual. Lythia let me go after the first night, and I wasn't even sure what had happened until I saw that news report. Then I knew they were setting me up, so I went after Lythia, but that Nagual was too strong. It trapped me again and didn't let me go."

This was almost too much to comprehend. *That* was why Half-Light had been framing Bane. He was a danger to the prophecy because he was trying to set Oliver free. "How?" Oliver asked. "How do I undo it?"

Bane smiled. "You won't believe what I did," he said, a note of his old cocky self returning. "Really, bro, you've got to see it to believe it. It's gonna blow your mind. But we have to go home first. I've got some things hidden back in my coffin that we need." He started to stand, but staggered. "Man, what was *in* that stuff I drank?"

"I don't know," said Oliver. "Désirée gave it to me."

Bane's face darkened. "Désirée?"

"Yeah, she said it would help you."

Bane looked unconvinced. "You can't trust her, bro. Not at all."

"But, Désirée's helped me figure out a ton of stuff."

"Did she? Well, it's only what she *wants* you to figure out, believe me." He staggered, wincing and clutching at his stomach. "Ahhh . . ."

"Whoa." Oliver caught him and put an arm around his shoulder.

"I got it, lamb," Bane said through gritted teeth, pushing himself away.

"Come on, idiot," Oliver snapped, slipping into old habits. "You need help."

Bane spun. "Idiot?" He raised his fist, only this time with a slight smile, and threw a punch at Oliver's gut.

Oliver tensed for the blow, and found himself almost looking forward to it, in a weird way. All this time, all his frustration with Bane, only to learn that his brother was on his side, was risking everything to save him.

But the punch never came.

"Whu —"

Oliver looked up to see Bane staring at him, eyes wide and glowing amber, his mouth open in shock. But he was changing — his face crystallizing. . . .

"Bane?"

As Oliver watched, his brother dissolved into dust.

CHAPTER 13

Dust, Tears, and Bones

"**N**o!" Oliver screamed.

Only an echo of Bane remained, his shocked face fading, the dust of his slain body drifting to the ground —

Only not. It began rushing away over the grass in a silver stream. Oliver followed it, and watched as it was gathered inside a small, red stone box —

In Lythia's hand.

"Thanks, Oliver!" she shouted triumphantly.

Beside her, the zombies held Dean and Emalie at the edge of the clearing. Jenette was trapped, thrashing about inside some kind of green energy sphere.

"Ashes to ashes!" Lythia went on gleefully. "And a brother in a box for Lythia!" She slapped the lid closed.

"Tsss!" Oliver sprinted toward her, lunging into the air, his eyes glowing in fury — he would slay her with his bare hands —

But Lythia's smirking face swirled into smoke as she evanesced, shooting up into the darkness. He landed on his knees where she had been.

The green sphere around Jenette faded. The zombies released Dean and Emalie and dashed off.

Dean spun to give chase, but Emalie grabbed his shoulder. "No, Dean," she said, turning back toward Oliver.

He scrambled around on the ground, looking wildly for — "Bane!" *My brother is gone.* "No . . ." Oliver moaned.

"Oliver," Emalie began. She put a hand on his shoulder.

Oliver slumped. That was it. He had no energy to move, ever.

But no — he lurched to his feet and ran.

"Oliver, wait!" Emalie shouted, but she let him go.

He had to move. Hurling himself through the trees, through blackberry bushes that tore at his hands, clothes and face . . . running . . . until finally he reached the bluff edge, where he collapsed to the ground in pain and anger, and some new, empty feeling like he'd never experienced before. He could only imagine that a human would call it sorrow.

❋

Oliver didn't know how long he sat with his head in his hands, but when he first noticed the light through the gaps in his fingers, he wondered seriously if it was dawn.

Let it be the sun, he thought. There was a slight hissing sound. *Let it burn me to dust.* He was almost disappointed when he remembered that the bluff faced west.

Besides, this light was different. White . . .

Oliver pulled his head up slowly. Below his dangling feet, the sound of lapping waves drifted softly through the fog. Oliver could see over the low, rounded banks of mist to the open water, where a large cargo vessel blinked, its engine churning. Beyond that, sleepy lights were clustered around the inlets of the far shore, and the snowcapped peaks of the Olympic Mountains were just visible in the moonless night. Oliver wondered at how peaceful the night was — indifferent to what had just happened.

Bane . . .

It wasn't hard to remember a time when Oliver might have smiled at the thought of his brother exploding into dust, getting what he deserved after all the annoying torment. But now Oliver felt like he was one of those bats in the zoo, only his cage had just been opened. In a single moment he'd learned that really, there was something much larger, with so many more possibilities — *a brother who was trying to help me all along* — only to have that cage door slammed closed in his face. He'd wondered if the animals were better off not knowing the world they were missing — the world they could never have. Maybe they were.

No! He didn't want to think about it anymore. It was all much worse than some thought about animals, much worse than anything he had ever felt, and maybe that surprised him most of all. Oliver didn't even know that feelings like this were possible for a vampire. And if they were, what did you do with them? What did you do with this horrible ball of empty pressing out against your guts?

Let me help.

Oliver reined his gaze back in from the far mountains. That wasn't Emalie's voice. He noticed that white light again that he'd mistaken for dawn. He turned, and found a glowing figure sitting beside him.

The apparition.

Hey, it said.

Its human shape was clearer than ever. The outline of jeans and sneakers and a sweatshirt. Of shaggy hair, but beyond the faint line of a nose and mouth, and the impression of eyes, the white glow made the face impossible to pick out.

Hey, Oliver said back.

Sorry about your brother, the apparition said.

Oliver didn't reply. He didn't know what to say or think.

Here, this will help.

The apparition pinched its forearm, its fingers sinking into itself. There was a bright pulse of white light, shooting sparks of blue, and it pulled a tiny sphere of itself free. It held this out to Oliver.

What is it? Oliver asked.

Between its fingers was a marble-sized sphere of glowing white. It was translucent, swirling like liquid. *It's part of me. For you.*

Oliver reached out and took the sphere between his thumb and first finger. It felt warm, squishy. *What do I do with it?*

Eat it.

What?

Oliver, you know you can trust me.

Strangely, Oliver felt certain that he could. He placed the sphere in his mouth.

And gagged. His body convulsed, tightening like a knot, his throat constricting, his eyes squinting shut, his guts flipping in on themselves.

Then he felt a huge release, a terrible, tearing feeling inside like a dam breaking. His body slumped, muscles failing, a great rushing sound in his ears. *"Tsssss!"* He screamed.

Silence.

Oliver's face fell to his hands. After a moment, he lifted his head and felt something strange on his palms. He looked down and saw streaks of water. He touched his cheeks below his eyes and found tiny rivers of liquid. A drop reached his mouth. It tasted salty.

What's happening to me? Oliver asked, confused.

They're tears, the apparition replied.

I'm . . . crying? He'd seen Emalie and other humans do this. It always looked so painful, so weak. It felt that way, too, yet strangely, the feeling was good. It was a relief. It didn't make what had happened to Bane any better, but maybe somehow it did.

It's called grief, the apparition added. *It heals.*

It ended in a moment. Oliver felt the tears cease, and almost wanted to ask for more. Instead, he asked: *What are you?*

He felt the apparition smile. *Soon.*

But I know you, don't I?

Yes. The apparition stood. *Something to show you, first.*

Oliver got to his feet. The apparition floated back into the bushes. Oliver followed, pushing more carefully through the blackberry with his already-torn hands. They passed between two crumbled mausoleums. Above, the first birds called in the predawn.

The apparition stopped. *Here.*

Two tombstones stood at angles, overgrown with vines.

Oliver reached down and brushed aside the leaves. Moldy, raised lettering read:

HOWARD BAILEY — 1923-1946
LINDSEY BAILEY — 1927-1946

Beside these was a small footstone.

NATHAN BAILEY — 1945-1946

"Oliver." Oliver turned to see Emalie, Dean, and Jenette emerging from the trees. "We've been looking for you," Emalie said. Oliver saw the puffy redness around her eyes, like she'd been crying, too. "I'm so sorry about Bane, I —" she trailed off at the sight of the gravestones.

"Is it them?" asked Dean.

Oliver nodded.

"How did you find them?" Emalie asked.

Oliver turned to point to the apparition, but it was nowhere to be seen. *You'll see me again,* it said to him from somewhere distant.

"It was here, wasn't it?" Jenette asked.

Oliver turned to her. "You've seen it?"

"Yes."

"What is it?" Oliver asked.

Jenette seemed to frown. "He told me not to tell you, yet."

"What are you guys talking about?" Dean asked.

"The apparition," said Oliver.

"I suppose you could call it that," mumbled Jenette.

Oliver's gaze returned to the stones. "Is it really them?"

"See for yourself," Jenette replied.

Oliver almost didn't want to. He felt so tired, so blank. The strange experience of crying left him wanting to curl up and sleep for days. But he dropped to his knees and started digging.

Emalie knelt beside him to help. Dean joined them.

Oliver filled his hands with soil and rocks, scooping it to the side. He hit a tree root and ripped it free. With each handful he dug faster. His nails filled with packed dirt; one tore away. He kept digging. Now that he was so close, he just wanted to know them, to touch the bones that had created his, to make up for the loss of Bane and share what little embrace he could with his parents.

When he hit wood, he raised his fist and punched through it. His hand entered a hollow space, and cracked against bones. Oliver grabbed at the jagged wood edges and tore them away, throwing aside the last barrier. He reached inside, clutching a handful of the cold hard bones, yanking them free.

Yet he already knew something was wrong — had known it from the second he broke through the coffin and caught a whiff of the old air finally freed — knew it fully when his fingers grazed the bones. Oliver looked at the bundle in his hand. They were curved: ribs that had once held the lungs and heart of a —

"Pig," said Oliver blankly.

"What?" asked Emalie.

Oliver grasped one bone tight and let the rest clatter back into the coffin. He turned it over in his hand. "This is the rib of a pig," he said. "Not a human. This . . ." He felt a rush inside. "These aren't my parents."

"But why a pig?" Dean asked.

Oliver's thoughts raced. "If you wanted to make a coffin feel like it had a human in it," said Oliver, putting the pieces together, "it's not a bad substitute."

"So," said Dean, "where are your parents?"

Oliver almost smiled. "Alive. Somewhere. Don't you think?"

Emalie nodded. "I *do* think . . . but what if you get your hopes up and it's wrong? I want us to be sure."

"Yeah," Oliver agreed. "It would be nice to be sure about something, for once. But how?"

"Why don't we go check out the night they died again?" suggested Dean.

Emalie and Oliver turned to him. "Huh?" Oliver mumbled.

"You know, and this time you could take me along."

"Oh." Oliver got it. "You mean the portal . . . to the night I died. Yeah, but we used that picture of me, and it got destroyed."

"It didn't though," said Emalie distractedly, her brow working on thoughts. "The negative is fine. I . . . I still have it in the basement. But we'd need a portal like Dead Désirée gave us."

"I really don't feel like asking her for another," said Oliver. Bane's words echoed in his mind: *Don't trust her.* And he pictured Bane's face turning to dust. "Wait," Oliver said.

"What?" asked Dean.

Oliver reached into his pocket and looked at the black bottle. "Just before Bane turned to d —" he couldn't quite get the word out. "He was complaining about this stuff. Like it was hurting him, but Désirée said it would make him feel better." Oliver looked at Emalie and Dean. "How did Lythia slay Bane?"

"She didn't," Emalie replied.

"Yeah," added Dean. "She caught us and was right beside us. She didn't throw out a stake or anything, just pulled out that box like she . . ."

"Like she knew it was about to happen," said Oliver darkly. Could it be true?

"You think Désirée's tincture slayed Bane," said Emalie.

Oliver could only nod.

"Dude," Dean mumbled.

"Does that mean Lythia and Désirée . . ." Emalie didn't finish.

A moment of silence passed over them. Oliver remembered thinking about how much Désirée had "helped" him. What had she really been doing? Toying with him? Using him? And for what? What were she and Lythia really up to?

"I guess that rules out asking Désirée for another amulet portal," said Dean.

"We don't need to," said Emalie resolutely. "I can make one."

"That's dangerous," warned Jenette.

Oliver eyed Emalie. She was still shaking ever so slightly. "Can you?"

"Yeah, pretty sure. I'll have to research the enchantment — have my Aunt Kathleen help me, but why not? It just might take awhile."

"Did you miss the part where it's dangerous?" Dean asked, concern in his voice, too.

"She can do it," Oliver said, locking eyes with Emalie. He needed her to. "We'll just have to be careful."

Oliver stood, looking down at the false graves, and felt a surge. His human parents were out there. He felt sure of it. Then he glanced around. His friends were with him, and they had a plan.

But my brother is gone.

The thought froze Oliver, and yet there was a sliver of calm inside him since the tears: *Bane was trying to save me.* It made the fact that he was gone so much worse, and yet, the thought also gave Oliver some kind of new feeling. He didn't know how to describe it.

And Bane had said that he'd found a way to undo the prophecy. There *was* a way. If Oliver could pick up where Bane left off, just as Oliver had picked up the prophecy where Bane had left off. . . . He could do this. They could do this. This new feeling was beginning to overtake him, to make him shake. Maybe it was just hunger and total exhaustion.

No, Emalie said in his mind.

Oliver found her clear eyes focused on him. *What is it, then?*

Hope.

Oliver nodded. "Yeah," he said aloud. Hope.

"All right, kids," Dean groaned. "If you guys are through, we should get subterranean." He glanced up into the trees, where the glimpses of sky had lightened to gray.

Oliver stepped out of the graves and pushed the dirt back in with his foot. Then he turned away, leading them through the trees. He felt a rush of worry as he imagined Phlox and Sebastian reacting to the news about Bane.

Bane . . .

That was going to be terrible, Oliver was certain of that. But he was certain of something else, too.

He would finish what his brother started.

Oliver's journey continues in

OLIVER NOCTURNE

#5: THE ETERNAL TOMB

Turn the page for a sneak peek...

We're in, Oliver thought.

Great. Emalie popped into sight between him and Dean.

They entered the cabin of the ship. Rows of seats were bent at odd angles, strung together with cobwebs. The floor was stained with rust and eaten through in places. The boat had been out of use for decades, and looked it, which was the point. No one would expect a meeting of such importance to be held here.

They reached a door and Oliver paused. He could hear the echoing voices on the other side.

He turned and shot a severe glance at Emalie and Dean.

"We know," Dean moaned, "stay quiet and don't get found out and all that."

"Pretty much," Oliver agreed.

"I just wish I could go." Dean pouted.

"I tried, Dean," Emalie said sympathetically.

"I know, I know. No way to make a lowly zombie invisible." Dean rolled his eyes. "It's safer anyway," he said, fingering the pendant around his neck. "Just in case . . ."

"Right," said Oliver.

"We'll tell you everything," Emalie promised.

"Have a great time," Dean grunted with a wave of his hand. "I'll be here keeping watch."

Emalie nodded and disappeared out of sight again.

Oliver felt for the forces and spectralized, disappearing as well. Then he turned and pushed open the door, and stepped through. There was no floor on the other side. Oliver steadied himself against the forces and slid onto a curved, metal wall.

You there?

Right beside you, Emalie thought back. *Wow.*

Thirty feet below them, at the base of sheer metal walls, were three perfect spheres of chairs facing center. Behind them, a ring of windows looked out into black water beneath the ferry. Magmalight globes swirled white-hot between the windows.

Every chair except for two was filled by a finely dressed vampire. All eyes faced center, to the circle of space occupied by two figures: Phlox and Sebastian. Oliver tensed at seeing his parents. They were the subject of this specially convened inquisition.

Phlox and Sebastian stood beside one another, shoulders touching. Oliver could practically feel the dark emotions coming off them. It was evident in their tight faces.

"Is there anything else you can tell us?" It was Tyrus McKnight, sitting among the circle.

"I think we've explained quite enough," Phlox replied indignantly. "We know nothing of what Bane was up to. He is —" her voice hitched, and her eyes began to glow turquoise, "*was* his own demon."

Oliver felt a knot forming in his stomach. This was the first reaction he'd seen from his parents about losing Bane. On that night, two weeks ago now, when Oliver had returned home, stood in the living room, and said, "Bane's gone," Phlox and Sebastian had barely moved. They'd been exhausted at the time, having spent many nights searching for Bane, not knowing until it was too late that Half-Light was framing him for a series of human murders. Oliver's awful news had only seemed to press them further into the couch.

Vampires didn't cry, or feel what a human would call grief. They expressed such feelings through rage and vengeance. When Oliver delivered the news, he'd expected a hideous explosion of curses and calls for vengeance against Lythia, Desiree, and even Half-Light, and yet . . . nothing. Oliver had waited. Maybe it would come the next evening, or the next. But the nights kept passing. Silent, tense, *empty*. Until now.

"There there, Phloxiana," a thin voice said below. It was Mr. Ravonovich, head of Half-Light, a wiry old vampire with ancient eyes, pure white skin, and razor sharp, parchment-colored teeth. "These are certainly unfortunate events."

"Why don't you tell *us* what Bane was up to?" asked Sebastian, his voice quiet, dangerous. "You're the ones who planned to slay him."

"What *we* planned to do, Sebastian," Ravonovich muttered in reply, "was whatever was necessary to protect the prophecy. We are here tonight to determine what *you* knew, not the other way around. And we have found that you were not aiding your son in his traitorous actions. Which is fortunate for us all. Now we must turn our attention to the future. The case of Bane Nocturne is closed. We have precious little time before the Darkling Ball, only a week remains, and we must assure that nothing jeopardizes the Anointment."

Is that about you? Emalie's thought echoed directly into Oliver's mind.

I think so.

All he knew was that this power was critical to him opening the Gate and freeing the vampires, which would also destroy the world and everything in it, including his friends.

"Once the Anointment is completed," Ravonovich continued, "there can be no stopping us. The prophecy can no longer be tampered with, and the Gate *will* be opened."

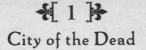